MISSION TO GEHENNA

SPEAR BOOKS SERIES

Sugar Daddy's Lover *Rosemarie Owino*
Lover in the Sky *Sam Kahiga*
Mystery Smugglers *Mwangi Ruheni*
A Girl Cannot Go on Laughing all the Time *Magaga Alot*
The Love Root *Mwangi Ruheni*
The Ivory Merchant *Mwangi Gicheru*
A Brief Assignment *Ayub Ndii*
A Taste of Business *Aubrey Kalitera*
A Woman Reborn *Koigi wa Wamwere*
The Bhang Syndicate *Frank Saisi*
My Life in Crime *John Kiriamiti*
Black Gold of Chepkube *Wamugunda Geteria*
Ben Kamba 009 in Operation DXT *David Maillu*
Son of Woman in Mombasa *Charles Mangua*
The Ayah *David Maillu*
A Worm in the Head *Charles K. Githae*
Twilight Woman *Thomas Akare*
Life and Times of a Bank Robber *John Kiggia Kimani*
Son of Woman *Charles Mangua*
A Tail in the Mouth *Charles Mangua*
My Life with a Criminal: Milly's Story *John Kiriamiti*
The Operator *Chris Mwangi*
Birds of Kamiti *Benjamin Bundeh*
Nice People *Wamugunda Geteria*
Times Beyond *Omondi Mak'Oloo*
Lady in Chains *Genga-Idowu*
Mayor in Prison *Karuga Wandai*
Son of Fate *John Kiriamiti*
Kanina and I *Charles Mangua*
Prison is not a Holiday Camp *John Kiggia Kimani*
Confessions of an AIDS Victim *Corolyne Adalla*
Comrade Inmate *Charles K. Githae*
Colour of Carnations *Ayub Ndii*
The American Standard *Sam DeSanto*

KARANJA WA KAN'GETHE

MISSION TO GEHENNA

Spear Books
Nairobi

Published by Spear Books
a subsidiary of
East African Educational Publishers Ltd.
Brick Court
Mpaka Road/Woodvale Grove
Westlands
P.O. Box 45314
Nairobi

ISBN 9966 46 421 2

Typeset by
Elite Computers Ltd.
Harambee Plaza
P.O. Box 75289
Nairobi

Printed by:
Sunlitho Limited,
P. O. Box 13939,
Nairobi, Kenya.

Dedicated to you all, sons of men,
Who bear passports to Hell,
Your ever insatiable curiosity,
Which attempt to sate,
Always culminates in vanity.

CHAPTER ONE

The darkness was solid. The silence was deathly. The sultry atmosphere reeked of the putrid odour of rotting vegetation and decaying cadavers.

Suddenly, lightning flashed across the horizon. In that instant, we discovered we were in the centre of a cemetery. Metal, stone and wooden crosses stuck out of the overgrowth. Simultaneously, we espied grotesque dark figures in rags and shaggy hair stealthily stalking us.

We blundered across the cemetery. Occasionally, we stumbled into a bush or crashed into a gravestone. It began to rain. Heavily. The breeze chilled us to the spine.

"Do you hear those voices?" I whispered hoarsely to Keega who was a few metres ahead.

"Yes," he replied, his teeth chattering with cold. We paused and listened.

"Earth to earth. Ashes to ashes. Dust to dust. Amen."

"Do you hear them?" I asked, shivering.

There was another flash of lightning. It was closely followed by frightening rumbling of thunder. In the distance, a tree fell and started burning. The downpour changed into a hailstorm.

"Come on Kimuri," Keega said urgently. "We've got to get out of here."

"I wonder where we're going."

"We'll find out once we're out of danger."

The voices behind us were now chanting obscenities and bellowing circumcision songs. At times they laughed or screamed like drunkards. They were still pursuing us. We accelerated. I panted for breath.

Suddenly, I jabbed my leg on the stump of a broken wooden cross on a grave.

"*Woi, Ngai!*" I cried out, pain surging through my spine to the base of my skull.

"What's wrong?" Keega asked. In his attempt to slow down to examine my injury, he slipped and tumbled into a puddle of turbid water.

"*Woi*, my leg," I groaned, steeling myself against the pain, to avoid fainting. "I've lost my leg, Oh God!"

Keega crouched next to me. He felt the wound with his fingers. Warm blood spurted from the broken vessels.

1

"This is serious, brother," he remarked. He ripped off my shirt sleeve. He tied it as a bandage to stop the bleeding.

"Whizz," I winced with pain as he tightened the bandage on the wound. He rolled up my trousers' leg to the knee.

"What's the time?" I asked.

He consulted his watch. It had stopped. He looked at mine.

"It's half past twelve. Can't tell whether p.m. or a.m., unless we assume the darkness implies a.m."

When the voices reached us, this time much closer, Keega grabbed my arm. I hastily hobbled beside him. The frenzied insults and curses pursued us.

"Who are they?" I enquired.

"Maybe *Ngoma* — Spirits of the dead."

"How did we come here?"

"It's a mystery to me."

"Oh, God."

Another flash of lightning revealed that we had left the cemetery. We were now moving through the forest. We could hear the chirping of insects, the laughter of hyenas and the roaring of lions in the distance.

"I feel awful," I gasped.

"Take heart, brother, we'll rest ahead."

"I …"

Suddenly, a rush of nausea seized me. My head reeled. It was only with an exertion of will that I stopped myself from losing consciousness. The pain made my leg throb violently. My entire body ached.

While Keega was holding me to prevent me from falling, a swarm of insects flashing yellow and green lights invaded us. Keega released his grip on me to protect himself. The insects burned and stung wherever they touched the skin. We screamed in horror and waved our arms in the air frantically. They got into our mouths, chocking us as we screamed. We were only saved by lying prostrate on the wet grounds. The insects passed over. A burning sensation built up on our skins wherever the insects had stung. Shortly, the skin started swelling.

"Jesus," Keega whined, "I am burning all over.""

"Man, it's worse for me with the rotten leg."

"What shall we do?"

"Let's keep on moving until we die."

2

I shuddered at the thought of death.

"Aren't we already dead?" I asked.

"No, not yet. Otherwise ..."

An army of mice attacked us. They nibbled at our ankles and calves. We kicked this way and that way, jumped, hopped and kicked berserkly in the dark, sometimes hitting tree trunks or stones. We screamed.

Our fear was intensified when our screams were answered with mad laughter from an unseen audience. Horrified beyond my wits, I ignored the pain in my leg and the burning body and raced blindly after Keega.

The next thing I realized, I was gamboling in the air, floating like a feather. I caught up with Keega and ran beside him. Eventually, we emerged from the edge of the forest, gasping for breath.

"Are you alright?" Keega asked absurdly.

"Are you alright?" his voice echoed all around us.

We looked at each other, bewildered.

The darkness had abated, giving way to a misty fog. There was enough light for us to see what lay a few metres ahead of us.

I looked at my companion and wept. I could hardly recognize him. His whole body was covered with red ripe sores. He was grossly bloated. His features were overly exaggerated.

Seeing my affliction, he muttered in a voice which sounded strange to me.

"You are in no better shape yourself. Please let us not waste our sympathies."

The land before us was sandy with short thorny shrubs and thick course grass.

"I suggest we keep on moving until we die. Now I don't care a whit!" I declared, moving forward despite the pain in my body.

"I wish I knew what all this means," Keega said.

"So do I."

We struggled with our aimless journey and managed to keep a number of kilometres between ourselves and the evil forest.

I was about to say something to Keega when I perceived an abrupt change in the weather. It became sultrily warm and the air heavy. There was a flash of lightning. Then the rumbling of thunder. This was presently followed by a strong whirlwind that ferociously shot gritty sand grains into the air. Some of them strafed us, inflicting pain. We sensed some inexpli-

3

cable presence hovering around us. Then a heavy voice downed our heads.

> *"Death is a permanent detention,*
> *Of the Soul in exile,*
> *From the loved ones,*
> *And the adversaries alike,*
> *In ethereal habitations,*
> *Where it bleeds,*
> *For want of mortal contact,*
> *Which it is eternally denied."*

Gradually the fog receded, exposing more realms of mystery to our horrified faces. There was an abrupt cacophony of weird sounds in the atmosphere. Horrified piercing noises, agitated ululations, shrieking, squalling, growling, yowling, hooting and sundry inexplicable heart-rending, frightful sounds.

My adrenalin shot up. My hair bristled at the back of my neck. My knees started knocking as if they had suddenly been loosened. I inadvertently urinated on myself. My friend, Keega, was in no better condition. We were both petrified and firmly rooted to the ground.

Just as if all this torture was not enough, a graveyard with a forest of crosses sprouted in front of us. The epitaphs on the gravestones were scribbled in cursive dark letters. The inscriptions were illegible from our distance. Some of the crosses were white-washed, though the plaster was now corroded with age and severe weather. The wooden crosses were worm-eaten. The whole expanse of the gravestone was covered with pale flowers and overgrowth.

From the devil knows where, a set of bones in semblance of a human skeleton landed with a thud in front of us. We tried to run away only to be confronted by yet a similar apparition. Any direction we turned, we saw nothing but skeletons. They were everywhere! This spectre was so terrifying and disarming that all we could do was to stand there, mesmerized and trembling with fear; our hearts in our mouths.

Gradually, one of the skeletons started gaining flesh. At first, ghastly rotten flesh with wriggling, fat maggots which gradually healed. In a matter of minutes, we stood face to face with an incredibly handsome youth. He was over six feet tall, strongly built with proportional features. He wore an amiable reassuring smile on his lips. Lack of an auriole precluded the

4

assumption that he might be an angel of God. Overcome with curiosity, we studied him with rapt interest.

He was clad in a long dark brown satin robe embroidered with glittering fold beads at the collar, on the sleeves and near the hem. He wore light magnificent sandals made from a serpent's skin. Round his wrist he wore a large gold-plated watch. His face was ageless.

He gave us enough time to study him before finally introducing himself.

"Sons of men, welcome to the Kingdom of Gehenna. I'm Satan Lucifer, the Sovereign. Follow me."

CHAPTER TWO

Wretched and helpless, we followed Satan through the wilderness, as sheep follow their master to the slaughterhouse. In the prevailing circumstances, we hoped, he was our only refuge and salvation.

The fog cleared. The setting of the sun cast its final glimmer on the northern horizon. I consulted my watch. It indicated 3 o'clock. In my confusion, I concluded there was something drastically wrong with my watch, or the order of time here was completely different from that of the Earth.

When I tried to comment, I realized I had lost my voice. My burning throat could only permit an inaudible whisper. I communicated this information to Keega through gestures. He, too, could not talk.

Satan walked briskly ahead of us. Our agony increased with our added effort to keep pace with Satan. We trudged on a sand strewn path that wound through dunes and precipices, via a clump of strange trees.

Our fear and suspicion resumed when wild animals came charging at us menacingly, only to retreat in humiliation when they recognized Satan. The whole land was haunted by serpents, djinn, forest spirits, carnivora and flying reptilia. A cruel and hideous principle of destruction assailed this new world.

Eventually we reached a broad river. Its tepid water exuded an offensive smell. Its surface was sprinkled with debris of leaves and grass. A miasma of decay hovered about it. The banks were slippery with green slime. The river flowed languidly. Almost imperceptibly.

"You must be tired after your tedious journey from the Earth," Satan observed. "You shall feel better after dipping yourselves in this river."

Keega and I exchanged worried glances. Surely this slime is enough to infect one with disease. I said within myself. And, who knows maybe even kill those who were already diseased like us. Moreover, we could not entirely rule out the idea of a trick. Probably he wanted to drown us. Or feed us to animals in the water.

I shook my head in disapproval.

"See, gentlemen," Satan insisted, "you have no choice. You either comply or your maladies will perpetually linger with you."

I looked down at my wound. Blood had seeped through the bandage.

6

It palpitated with pus. Our bodies were covered with sores, bruises, cuts and mud.

Sensing my plight, Satan took hold of my leg. I flinched with pain as he wrenched off the bandage. The wound had already turned septic. White worms wriggled in it. My head swam. I was too weak to resist the baptism. Satan dipped me in the filthy water seven times. When I emerged from the water the seventh time, I was already a new creature. Drenched to the skin, covered with grime but feeling better! I recovered my voice. My sores vanished. My wound healed. My fear drained. My spirit revived.

"Just what you need, man." I encouraged Keega, who just stood there awestruck. "Look at me, brother."

Reluctantly, he capitulated. He, too, was dipped into the river seven times and emerged, borne again.

"Yeah, men," he said gleefully, "I feel better."

"Thank you, sir," we said in unison.

"My pleasure," Satan replied.

Strangely enough, in such a short time, we felt as if we had always been acquainted with Satan. Presently, we found ourselves bombarding him with questions. Like a father to his inquisitive children, he answered them all without the slightest nuance of impatience or annoyance.

"What do you call this river, sir?" I enquired.

"The River of Death."

"Why?"

"Because," Satan replied, "all spirits of the dead have to cross it before taking their ultimate abode in Hell."

"Sir, Keega asked, "Why is the water so refreshing?"

"It contains certain chemicals which react with your skin and blood. This soothes you, releasing you of fatigue and all physical ailments. You regain your vitality, composure, poise and equanimity. These are all vital if your body is to stay healthy and strong. Once you attain this state of equilibrium, you experience no more pain. No more sorrow. No more fear."

"Thank you, sir," we repeated, really feeling grateful.

"Oh, you're welcome."

Satan's voice was enticing. We wished he could go on speaking. That modulated tone. That lilt. That captivating smile. Looking at Satan Lucifer there before us, I began to doubt the authenticity of the doctrine that Satan

7

was evil. I felt as if I could now stand, if given the chance, and recant all that I had learnt about Satan, both in church and at school. I could even vouch for him. I could stand and unabashedly tell the world:

"Satan is good!"

I looked up and saw him smiling at me shyly.

"Excuse me sir," I said, "back on earth we are told that only sinners gain admittance to Gehenna. Are we here because of our sins? If so, what's our fate?"

"Well, now, my dear Kimuri," Satan answered, "Sin is a delicate subject. What is sin in one community may be acceptable in another, see?"

I nodded, still expecting him to continue. He did.

"Sin may be defined as violation of certain ethical rules — religious or social. But you see rules differ with communities, religious traditions and education. One man's meat, another man's poison sort of thing, see?"

I nodded.

"To discount that only sinners visit Hell, another name for Gehenna, you only need to reflect on your Apostles' Creed. Jesus descended into Hell for three days. And Jesus was an honourable man."

"Our fate?" Keega prompted.

"You needn't be unduly alarmed," he assured us. "Most of what you hear on Earth is mere fantasy and has no ground. Your stay will be short and, I hope, very illuminating. You shall return to Earth in due course."

I rather liked that. Satan saw my contentment and smiled.

"I'm afraid we'll have to cut this interview short. You'll, however, have all the time to ask me your questions later. For now let's go home."

We were mysteriously lifted by an unseen force across the enormous river.

"Wonders of Gehenna!" I exclaimed as we landed on the other side.

"World without end," Keega rejoined.

"Everlasting kingdom," Satan added, giving us an enigmatic smile.

We climbed a hill with huge, smooth weather-beaten rocks that stood precariously on its slopes, then down a cliff.

* * *

The Mausoleum was a great octagonal pagoda with superimposed storeys surmounted by a spire. In all corners of the tiers hung multicoloured

8

electric bulbs. All around it were projections of houses. The tower was so exquisite and would easily outshine the Porcelain Tower of China of the fourteenth century. It looked antique and must have definitely cost a lot of money and labour. This in itself, I thought, portrayed ambitious egoism.

We marvelled at its magnificence. The pillars of each porch were made of white marble. The front rows were covered with gold plates reminiscent of Solomon's Temple in Jerusalem, prior to its destruction by Roman soldiers in the first century A.D.

We stopped at a wicket gate with a narrow door in it. From within, there was a sudden roaring of beasts. Fear seized us again.

"Calm down," Satan said reassuringly, "It's alright."

The gate opened automatically. We were in. Instead of entering the house through the front main door, or taking an elevator up, we once again felt ourselves mysteriously transported into space only to land on the porch of the seventh storey.

Keega and I exchanged glances, too baffled for words.

"We're home" Satan announced.

The palour was commodious. There were enormous divan seats, rocking chairs, round tables with satin and velvet cloths and flower pots.

In one corner there was a large chest of books with many volumes on all subjects. There were various versions of the Bible, Apocrypha, the Koran, Avesta and the Satanic Bible which was also simply referred to as 'The Book'.

"Come on, fellows. Sit down. Feel at home," Lucifer said cordially.

Our reflections in the wall mirrors reminded us of our true condition. We were a sorry sight. Wet and wrapped in rags and grime. We became even more embarrassed when we heard peels of feminine laughter from another part of the house.

"Thank you, sir," we said politely and sat on the edge of one of the seats, afraid of soiling it.

Satan pressed a button on his watch. Right behind him, a magnificent throne emerged. It glittered in the light. The seat was made of live tongues of fire which glowed red. As he sat in it, we expected him to burn. Nothing happened. He sat comfortably.

"I see you are impressed by my Hot Seat," Satan remarked. "The frame is made of pure gold."

He pressed another button on the table and the room was filled with music.

9

"Don't worry," he consoled, "You'll soon get used to the place."

"Excuse me, please," Keega croaked, then cleared his throat. "Where can I go for a short call?"

"Well, well," Satan said, picking up a wooden box, the size of a cigarette case from the table.

"You don't have to. If you feel pressed for elimination just take a pill from this box and it'll be over. That's all."

I gaped at him in wonderment.

Oh, yes, Kimuri, he reaffirmed. For your information things here work differently from those on Earth. We have no need for toilets or sanitary."

"I hope it's possible for us to wash off this grime? We're stinking like corpses," Keega ventured.

"Certainly, Mr. Keega."

He pressed a button on the table. The door on the far right side of the parlour opened. We found ourselves staring at a pretty Asian lady who stood there smiling genially, all wrapped in a bright red sari.

"Lubaina will show you the bathrooms," Satan said.

We joined her at the door. She allotted us the bathrooms.

"Kimuri," she cooed pointing to a door. "Keega," she pointed at a second bathroom.

We bathed in the refreshing warm water, shaved and dressed in the new clothes which were neatly folded and laid on a table. Lubaina patiently waited in the corridor.

"Thank you very much," I said to her. She acknowledged my gratitude with a smile.

"You look very elegant in your new suits," Satan complimented.

"Thank you, sir," we chorused.

Presently, another beautiful lady emerged from another door, carrying a big tray of food. It was just as if we were in a dream where most things cannot be explained immediately.

"Trixy Waruo," Satan introduced her.

The lady raised one leg in the air as they do in striptease shows. This, we learnt later, was their method curtsying in Gehenna. She served the food and left. She had a graceful walk.

The food was convivial. The meat tender. The blood delicious. We ate in silence. Much as we ate, the food seemed to remain at the same level as if it were not being consumed.

As we ate, my eyes roved around the walls. All around, there were human skulls which glowed like electric bulbs. On one wall there hung an amorphous map of Gehenna with its various oceans, seas, mountains and states.

I found myself wondering if Trixy was Satan's wife. If she were, why did he not introduce her as such?

I feared that if I asked him he might suspect my intentions. In African traditions, we don't rush into things until the most appropriate time. When we were full, Trixy came back and silently cleared the table.

No sooner had she left than Lubaina came with a tray containing glasses and a big chalice full of wine and another one full of fruit juice. She curtsied like Trixy and put the trays on the table.

"This, gentlemen," Satan announced, "is Lubaina Igbo. She was an Arab."

"Was?" Keega asked.

"Yes. In the Herebefore."

"And Waruo, I mean Trixy?" the question escaped from my mouth.

"Oh, yes, Kimuri, I see you've already taken fancy of her. I didn't tell you. She was obviously Kenyan. I'm sure, Kimuri, you have heard about her. Trixy Waruo, a queen of beauty and the first woman graduate from your village. She is still talked about. She disinfected her mother-in-law before admitting her into her house. She murdered her wealthy husband over insurance premiums. The Insurance firm investigated and uncovered the plot. She committed suicide before the police arrived.

Keega and I exchanged furtive glances.

"I've heard of her," I said.

Before Lubaina poured wine into my glass I protested. "No, thanks," I said. "I don't take alcoholic beverages."

"Neither do I," Keega joined in.

She served us fruit juice and left.

"But why, gentlemen?" Satan demanded. "A little alcohol in moderation is good for health. It helps you forget your troubles and wipes off bad memories."

"Yes, sir," I agreed, "But I believe it's better for one to refrain from all habits that might lead one into unnecessary problems."

"What do you mean?"

"Once a habit is formed, it is hard to break it."

11

"Why should one want to break it, anyway?"

"Financial difficulties, poor health, or shortage of commodities."

"That's the trouble with you, human beings," he remarked, "You worry yourselves unnecessarily. At any rate, feel free here. You won't have the problems you've just mentioned."

"Thank you, sir, but one still needs to look before one leaps", I argued.

"That's human wisdom. Anyway, it's all up to you," he shrugged.

"Okay then, maybe if you don't drink you smoke?" He looked at us questioningly.

"Here we have bhang, cigarettes, cheroots and cigars all at your disposal."

He put a small carton box on the table. We just stared foolishly at the stuff.

"Okay guys," Satan said laughing sardonically, "Relax. You'll soon get used to life here." ·

Our bewilderment was enhanced by the emergence of two new ladies into the parlour.

The white one was tall with a trim body. Her hair was dyed copper-red and glittered in the light. It fell freely and spread on her shoulders. She wore a thin Tee-shirt, behind which I could see the outline of her untethered breasts. She was tattooed on the arms, on the thighs and all parts of the body that were not covered by her scanty clothing. She had large blue eyes.

Her companion was shorter and beautiful in her own way. Her curly hair was well groomed and coiffered in an Afro-style. She had painted her eye lids with eye shadow. Her brown skin aptly received calculated attention. Both women wore bikinis that revealed their well rounded thighs and supple hips.

"Chattel Kamali," Satan announced. The shorter lady raised her leg and one arm in the air.

"Gloria Gallows."

The white lady did the same.

"They'll usher you to your bedrooms. Good night."

"Good night and thank you, sir" Keega and I chorused. We bowed in deference before Satan, then left.

In the corridor, the two ladies clasped us, each embracing her partner vociferously. We stopped — to kiss. Gloria almost dragged me down with her, kissed me wetly, passionately, whining and whimpering hungrily

12

under her warm breath.

"That's enough for now, G.G," I said pushing her away. "Show me my bedroom."

At this, she grabbed my hand. We ran like mad and burst into a room with an enormous golden bedstead and a dressing table. Before I had even surveyed the room she was already on me, tearing off my clothes. Her eyes smouldered with demonic lust, her body spasming with electric current.

We struggled and wrestled. She would have overpowered me if I hadn't hit her, hard. She left, but not before exhausting her stock of invectives. She swore that soon she would get me.

CHAPTER THREE

The night was terrible. I could hardly sleep. My brain seethed with anger, bitterness and hatred. For a long time I stood in the middle of the room staring at the wall without focusing, lost in thought.

Admittedly, we found Satan Lucifer with his retinue of sex-crazed women quite a curious lot. How and why we were here remained a mystery to me. Besides, it was difficult to know what to expect. Despite Satan's assurance, I still feared for our safety. What, I wondered, was the big idea behind his tempting us with alcohol, drugs and women? Suddenly I felt lonely and hollow. I wished my friend, Keega, were with me so that we might grapple with these problems together. Realizing that my thoughts were not getting my anywhere, I jerked my mind to the immediate reality.

I paced round the room, studying the pornographic mural on the walls. They protrayed men, women, children and breasts embroiled in mass sexual orgies. On the sideboards were obscene curvings and sculptures made of marble. A glass cabinet at one corner contained glasses and bottles of a variety of strong drinks.

I stopped at the bookshelf and inspected the titles. Most of the books were on crime, sex, adventure and travel. I noticed some popular authors such as Alan Edgar Poe, Dennis Whitley, Amos Tutuola, Pushkin and Bran Stoker. The rest were on voodooism, witchcraft and sorcery. I picked up an anthology of poems on ghosts and demons. I read a few pages. I found them too horrifying. I returned the book. As my whole body was overcome by malaise and my mind utterly exhausted, I ensconced myself in the warm and comfortable bed and tried to force myself to sleep.

* * *

I must have dozed off.

Suddenly, weird noises jolted me awake. It was a ferocious howling wind that nearly shook the building off its foundations. Gradually, it abated. I felt a cold mist seeping in through the wind. Then, somebody moving in the room. My spinal column turned icy with fear. I held my breath and listened.

For some time I heard only the thumping of my heart. I thought I had imagined it. Then somebody gave out a long sigh. This confirmed my fears.

A chair shifted from the table and came to rest near the bed. I abruptly sat up, trembling. I could feel the skin on the back of my neck crawling. Whoever was in the room was definitely enjoying my predicament.

The drinks cabinet opened. Two glasses filled with whisky. They drifted on the bedside table.

"How about a drink, mate?" the intruder whispered.

I shook my head, too shocked to scream.

One glass rose in the air. The contents disappeared. The other one followed suit. The two glasses were then abruptly shattered on the ground. The invisible visitor joined me in bed. I felt ice-cold lips lustfully sucking mine. I smelt whisky fumes in her breath. An enormous bust pressed against me. A cold hand with long nails fumbled with my groin. I fainted.

The next morning I was all alone in bed; stark naked. I sprung up, put on my clothes and looked at myself in the mirror. My features appeared haggard. My face was drawn. My eyes were red from lack of sleep. They carried heavy pouches underneath them. My mind was dazed with confusion.

The door was violently kicked open and Gloria stood there grinning at me.

"Hi, Kimuri," she cooed, obviously in a jovial mood.

"What do you want?" I growled, unable to conceal my apprehension.

"Come on, dearie, it's time for breakfast. Our Lord, Satan Lucifer, is waiting for you chaps. Don't lose your temper, it's precious. Now hurry up while I call Keega."

"Welcome, gentlemen," Satan greeted us when we came into the parlour.

"Relax. You don't have to be morose, do you?"

"No, sir," we said, not knowing what else to say.

"You must learn to inure yourselves to many occurrences here, which will appear quite unusual to you. It's the only way you may enjoy your stay here."

We toyed with our breakfast like new prisoners do with their first prison gruel. We had no appetite. Satan pretended not to notice. Each time he looked at me, I would avert my eyes. He ordered for brandy to be served. This time we did not resist. The drink gave us back our composure and helped us to relax. Lovely music played softly in the background.

15

"Gentlemen, I'm sure you'll enjoy your stay here. Remember there are no inhibitions. You'll find the ladies most charming. Feel free to indulge in all your fancies. Everything is at your disposal. No cause for alarm. You'll be closely protected from any grave dangers. Is that clear?"

"Yes sir," we replied readily.

"Certainly, you would be interested in exploring my kingdom. You'll meet two gentlemen at the gate. They'll be your guides."

Fumbling with his breast pocket, he produced two capsule tablets.

"After swallowing these, no wild animal should bother you. But don't provoke them."

"Thank you, sir," Keega's voice joined mine in the expression of our gratitude.

"I have other matters to attend to. We shall meet later. Have a good time."

At the porch, Lucifer ordered us to leap down from the brink. Despite our fear that we might be jumping to our deaths, we found ourselves smoothly floating in the air like two air denizens, ultimately landing gingerly on the ground below.

"Boy you talk of places! Believe me, this is the strangest of them all," Keega remarked as we walked towards the gate.

"I couldn't agree with you more," I rejoined.

"Would you believe that I suspected that the benevolent Lucifer would turn into Count Dracula at night?"

"And did he?"

"By Jingo! I forgot all about it. How can you remember anything when insatiable nymphos decide to rape you and, before you know it, you have already been overcome by sleep?"

"My Goodness! I thought sexy ghosts only haunted girls' boarding schools."

"Now you know better."

I looked at him questioningly. Then we both burst out laughing.

Outside the gate, plants stretched out enthusiastically toward the morning sun. Their various scents mingled in consonance, synthesizing into a peculiar, exotic perfume that pervaded the air, making it all the more pleasant to inhale.

A variety of insects, some with sharp shrieks like high tuned musical instruments, frolicked from one flower to the next, sucking nectar with

16

relish and transporting pollen grains. The insects were singularly fascinating to watch.

The two guides waited for us at the end of the hedge. Their skins had a peculiar ashen colour which made it difficult for one to know whether they were black, brown, coloured or white. The distinction could be inferred from the texture of their hair and the colour of their eyes but that, too, could be misleading.

"I'm Major Gakuu," the shorter of the two said.

"Challenge Graves," the other one rasped curtly.

"I'm Kimuri and my companion is Keega," I said.

"Has he no mouth to speak for himself, or is he dumb?" Challenge asked rudely.

"You're from the Earth?" Gakuu asked dismissing Challenge's flippant questions.

"Yes," Keega replied. "To be precise, we're from Kenya."

"I hate niggers!" Challenge scoffed.

"That's great," Gakuu said beaming with pleasure. "I also came from there."

"Sons of men are mad," Challenge rasped with a scowl, his manner expressing disgust.

We did not see the point in his bullying us. Probably it was he who was mad. We concluded that Challenge was not likeable and it would be very difficult to get along with him. We, therefore, decided it would be wise to keep quiet and report him to Satan. I liked Major Gakuu at once.

He was a short thickset man with thick lips. His skin was as hairy as a gorilla's. He wore a dirty brown singlet, brown flannel trousers and a fading blue levis jacket.

His companion, Challenge Graves, was about six feet tall, hunky with shag-cut long black hair, stubbly bearded. He was better dresses. He wore green slacks and a rust-coloured sports jacket. He never laughed nor smiled. For a smile he always managed a smirk. His green eyes had something deeply disquieting about them — a drowsy quality which suggested easily eruptible violence.

Both were drunk. They exuded the smell of gin from their clothes and breath. We noticed that all inhabitants of Gehenna, except those in Satan's domicile, spoke in rasping voices.

We later learnt that Challenge was fond of making boorish, practical

17

jokes on all his friends and acquaintances. This abominable habit had got him into several scuffles in which he had killed three people.

We moved through a country with unfamiliar landscape. The trees, the creepers and the grass all looked different from those we were used to back on earth. There were plants with black flowers and twisted roots that grew above the soil like rudimentary legs.

We climbed steep hills by a tortuous path which was flanked by huge lofty rocks which hang dangerously on its sides. From the top, we surveyed the countryside.

From here we could see Poverty Mountains and Economy Mountains further on to the east with their snowcapped peaks jutting into the cumulus clouds.

In the Plains of Deceit we could see the vast Ignorance Sea with its cluster of islands; Prince Chaos Islands and, the largest of them, the Blindfaith Islands.

Gakuu pointed out to us the direction of the Oceans of Fantasy, Oblivion Ocean, the Questioning Mountains, Sea of Doubts, Inflation Crator, Carnal Lust Plains and the State of Diseases; which we could not see from our position.

In the forest, some trees molested us. They would calmly wait for us to approach then they would seize us and squeeze us out of breath. Others would lash out at us and send us scampering in all directions, screaming. Challenge seemed to enjoy our suffering immensely.

In other areas we came across volcanic cones emitting sulphurous substances that nearly choked us to death. Occasionally, the white embers scattered in the atmosphere, burning holes in our clothes. By the time we left this region, we were infested with acne and our faces were full of pimples.

No sooner had we left one area than we found ourselves entangled in more terrifying situations. In some places, we had encounters with malignant spirits and djinn. They were full of mettle and mischief. They competed in trying their evil stints on us. The Spirit of death challenged us into duels. The Spirit of lust charged us with all sorts of carnal desires. It urged us to gratify them by all available means — homosexuality or sodomy.

There were all sorts of Spirits. The Spirit of hatred. The Spirit of jealousy. The Spirit of rebellion. The Spirit of prodigality. The Spirit of

18

greed. All inexorably vying to put us under their clutches.

Down in the valley, we came across a swiftly moving stream with crystal clear, cold water. We washed our faces and drank some water. Our two guides preferred to drink their liqueur which they carried in round encased flasks.

We picked and ate the fruits that grew there in profusion. There were huge juicy oranges, mangoes, paw-paws and wild red bananas. Whether some of the other unfamiliar fruits were edible or not, we had yet to learn. Gakuu warned us that there were some among them that were deadly poisonous, while some could easily drive one mad if one ate them.

Occasionally we frightened packs of hares, mice and lemmings en route. We noticed that they were by far larger than those of the Earth.

There were warning cries from frightened birds here and there as we approached their secret homes in the grass.

Then, as if on cue, we heard discordant hooting from a choir of owls and owlets. Keega and I exchanged suspicious glances. We were both visibly shaken.

"What's the matter?" Gakuu enquired.

"It's the owls," Keega explained. "Their hooting portends death."

"Shit!" Challenge interjected. "Africans are full of superstitions!"

"There is no community without superstitions," I countered.

"And what the rot is that to me?" Challenge spat contemptuously.

So far, we had disliked Challenge's sarcastic talk and had deliberately ignored him. The only time when we could not help betraying our amusement was for a brief moment when he and Gakuu talked about their escapades in Destruction City where they lived.

Major Gakuu had recounted his experiences the previous night at a drinking place. The trite debates, and the scuffles. He had got himself stupidly drunk. When he woke up in his bed, he was surprised to find an unbelievably old woman beside him. He had made love to her all night long convincing himself she was a young girl. His anger flared up when the hag demanded a staggering fee for her unbegrudged services, at gun point. Gakuu had to comply.

Then Challenge proudly narrated an incident when a boy's father had caught him red-handed indecently assaulting the boy. A brawl had ensued. He slashed his assailant in the belly. His entrails gushed out. He died. The enraged tormentor slew the boy, too and fled.

19

"Now, Mr. Graves," Major Gakuu intervened. "It's unbecoming to talk to our Lord's guests like that."

"Shut up! Challenge bellowed, clenching his fists. His eyes smouldering with diabolic lust for violence.

"You must be mad," Gakuu retorted.

"I'll kill you, you idiot!" Challenge stammered nasally, resolutely advancing towards Gakuu.

We watched in amazement.

Gakuu retreated. His face distorted with fear. Challenge shot out his fist, clubbing Gakuu on the mouth. He spat out blood and two of his front teeth.

The sight of blood drove Gakuu mad. He rained a flood of blows and kicks at his opponent. Challenge was, for a moment, taken by surprise. His nose-bridge was severed and he bled profusely. Gakuu continued hammering him, his arms working like pistons.

We applauded and cheered him. After all, wasn't he protecting us from this murderer? His success, however, was short-lived. Challenge flew into the air like a tornado and gave Gakuu a flying kick on the chest, sending him sprawling helplessly to the ground. Before he could rise to his feet again, Challenge was on him kicking, slapping, biting, bruising him on the face, then mercilessly strangling him.

The hooting of the owls became more frenzied. Some inexplicable force impelled me to go to Gakuu's aid. I grabbed Challenge by the arms. I struggled to pull him off Gakuu before he hurt him further. He was stronger than I. He released his right arm from me in one swipe and, like a stallion, gave me a kick between my legs. I drew back holding my genitals.

"You, devil!" I cursed.

Keega rushed to our aid. Picking a thorny branch that had fallen from a nearby tree, he belaboured Challenge on the head soundly. He dropped from Gakuu, clasping the back of his head with hands that were full of bruises. Blood spurted from the wound on the head. Before he could rise up, and, before we could believe our eyes, Gakuu, his face beyond recognition with blood, had pulled out of his pocked a strange object. He pressed a button. A long blade of a knife shot out.

"Please don't …" I intoned, too late.

Major Gakuu was on Challenge Graves, stabbing him on the neck,

20

chest, belly, and on the face.

"Die, you cursed bastard," Gakuu said, rising from the limp body.

"Gosh! Why did you do that?" Keega asked in horror.

"The bugger asked for it," Gakuu replied, simply.

"But that now puts us in greater trouble."

I supported Keega, equally perplexed.

"It's alright. Come on, let's go!" Gakuu ordered.

The whole episode affected our temperaments drastically. Our immediate desire was to get away from this scene. Maybe return to Satan's palace and recuperate from the shock. I looked at the inert body of what was only a few minutes ago Challenge Graves. Nausea seized me.

"Yeah, Let's go." I echoed Gakuu.

"No!" Keega's sorrowful voice stopped me. "Let's bury him under that tree."

"Indeed." I agreed, going back to help him.

"No." Gakuu Shouted authoritatively.

We looked at him in bewilderment.

"Don't bother yourselves. The vultures will do a clean job on the corpse. As for the bones, leave that to the hyenas. Now let's go."

Gakuu wiped blood from his hands using the dead man's jacket. From one of its pockets he took out some money which he also put in his own pockets.

"Certainly he won't need this any more," he remarked.

We walked back with drawn faces. Silent. Each person immersed in his own thought. I was wondering. Why should man have so little regard for human life? Has civilization blunted man's feelings so much that he treats his fellow men as mere things to be used and discarded at will? Did they have anything like a 'Declaration of Human Rights' here?

Although I personally did not like Challenge, since our meeting, I was profoundly disturbed by his death. This increased my concern about our security, in spite of Satan's repeated assurance. Why did he care, anyway, if he did not only want to keep us off guard? Keega too, looked pertubed. I wished I could probe his mind. Yet, we couldn't freely discuss the matter while one of the Devil's disciples was with us.

When we got to the Mausoleum, we were tired, sweaty and dirty. We parted with Gakuu where we had met with the late Challenge Graves that morning.

"What do you think is going to happen?" I asked Keega as we moved towards the gate.

"Honestly, I don't know," he replied, "It's a murder case and I don't expect it to be very easy. I suggest we report the matter to Satan at once. Supposing this man, Gakuu pins this murder on us?"

"Definitely, it would be very difficult to exonerate ourselves. But then what do we do?"

"Well, nothing. Let us still tell him the truth, whatever happens."

At our approach, the gates automatically opened. We walked in. We were contemplating knocking at the front door when we saw Satan gazing down at us from the seventh storey.

"Come on up, men," he beckoned us.

Presently, we found ourselves mysteriously swept in the air, then delicately landing on the porch.

"I hope you had a magnificent time," Lucifer said with a friendly smile.

"Yes, sir," we answered.

"But why, you look troubled," he observed.

Keega could hardly wait until we sat down. He informed Satan what had happened to Challenge.

"Okay, fellows, relax. Now that you've got it off your systems don't let it bother you anymore," Satan said deprecatingly.

We were not satisfied. How could a serious matter like this be dismissed with such levity?

"Is there no law here? Is there no police force to maintain law and order?" I asked naively.

"My dear, Kimuri, this is Gehenna," Satan Lucifer reminded us. Supernatural law still remains nebulous and ambiguous to man. Human law is merely a body of conventional rules. Everybody here wants to live and be free. Then, it follows that if you don't kill, it is you who'll get killed. If you don't cheat, it's you who'll get cheated. Now, shall we have lunch?"

He pressed a button. Trixy Waruo and Chattel came in with trays of streaming ambrosia. They curtsied in their manner, served out the food and gave us quick salacious smiles before they left.

The second button filled the room with psychedelic amusement. We then washed our throats with wine. It had a soothing effect on us.

"Now, what you need is a good rest to help the food to settle in your

22

stomachs," Satan said, permitting an amiable smile.

"He is strange," I said in my mind. "Isn't he lulling us to sleep only to evade questions?"

When I looked up, Satan was curiously eyeing me, the smile still hovering on his lips.

"Wrong, Kimuri," he said. "Just relax and wait."

I was astonished that he could read my mind so easily. I refrained from any more conspiratorial thoughts.

Instead of taking our siesta in bed, Satan suggested we lie on the couches. On pressing at the edge of the seas, they spread out into vast comfortable beds.

"I'll be seeing you later," Satan said.

The music continued playing softly, in the background. In my vain attempt to fathom what all this meant, I fell asleep.

CHAPTER FOUR

Keega's frantic cries awoke me. I hastily looked around in alarm. Satan Lucifer was sitting on his throne, reading a magazine titled *Fate*. He gave me a wry smile as I jerked from the couch. Keega was talking in his sleep.

"Yeah! Why should I lie? It's real blood! You touch. Smell it. You see? It's even congealing on your finger. No!" he screamed in a falsetto tone. "Not me! Honestly I didn't kill him. Believe me. Why, I wouldn't even hurt a louse. What would I gain? Stop, you witch! No, Please. he..l..p!"

He woke with a start, his body wet with perspiration.

"What were the witches doing to you, Keega?" Lucifer teased.

"It was only a dream, sir."

"Tell us about it."

"They were slaughtering Challenge. They took out his heart, kidneys, liver and his manhood. They wanted to do the same to me. I woke up."

"Very interesting," Satan smiled sardonically.

"Horrible, sir," Keega corrected disconsolately.

I looked at him pitifully.

"If you are interested, I'll take you round the complex," Satan announced after tea.

Trixy came back to clear the trays. I found myself staring at her, mesmerized. It was Keega's laughter which made me pull myself together with some effort.

"Got to check this absurd habit," I reproached myself inwardly.

"It's alright Kimuri," Satan said. "There's no need for repression. Feel free. Stare if you want. Indulge if you can't control yourself. Now, fellows, shall we go round?"

Once again I was embarrassed by Satan's ability to read my mind. I felt that he already knew too much about us. More than we could guess. Yet he still managed to keep aloof and remained mysterious.

We were still bound by human morality. A sense of modesty required that we should respect those who were senior and elderly. To appear and sound promiscuous in thought, word or deed was one sure way of violating this rule. One was free to joke or share one's intimate secrets with one's age-mates. But Satan was not our age-mate. He was our host and superior. Besides, we hardly knew him well enough to know the extent to which we could be free with him.

24

We accompanied him into the vast kitchen. A room with comfortable dark furniture. On one of the chests was a huge closed circuit television. Wherever a button was pressed in the living room, the television came on. Then the message would be communicated. The receiver clearly seeing the sender.

In the preparation of meals, the maids operated knobs and switches that controlled solar energy in the containers. They would then time the food with the help of chronometers and reduce the heat and pressure when it was ready to be served.

Gloria demonstrated how all this was done. We watched with awe. The refrigerators, too, used the same system of temperature control devices. This way they were able to retain food at the required temperature for as long as necessary. There were many other appliances in the kitchen, including dishwashers and two robots designed to look like women with plastic skins to help the maids with their work.

From there we visited the bedrooms. They all contained enormous luxurious golden bedsteads, bookshelves and drinks cabinets. Satan pointed out to us more switches, buttons and cords; explaining the purpose of each.

Simply by pressing the button, it was possible to watch films on the wall while lying in bed. Another switch would fill the room with music through stereophonic speakers concealed in the ceiling. It was also possible to change the temperature of the room by turning a dial to the required degree in centigrades. You could switch on lights or cause darkness by touching a knob on the wall.

In case one wanted to commit suicide, all one had to do was to pull a red cord and the air in the room would be suffused with mustard gas, carbon dioxide, mercuric oxide, chlorine or nitrogen oxide. If one did not consider that method comfortable enough, then one could pull another cord and all the air in the room would be exhausted. One would then die of suffocation. Keega and I exchanged quick suspicious glances.

Every bedroom had a bathroom attached to it. The walls were covered with mirrors. One could take a shower, a bath or a sauna bath. There was an array of creams, lotions, shampoos, skin ointments and hair oils. We marvelled at all the extravagance. Surely even Marie Antoinette with all her prodigality after embezzling state funds could not have been a match for Satan. I wondered at whose expense all this grandeur was attained.

The study was by no means less significant. It was a commodious

25

room with strange machines and huge bookshelves with forests of books, like a publishing firm. There were all sorts of books. Copies of the books in our bedrooms and Satan's parlour were also available here in several sets.

You could pick a book from the shelf, place it in a box, sit in a chair, put on earphones, then press a button on top of the box. An articulate voice read the book into your ears, explicitly pronouncing the beginning of each new chapter just about to be read. We were highly impressed.

There was another machine into which you spoke and all that you said was typed on a computer sheet. This machine was known as 'phonigraph'. It could produce several copies of the same material. All you had to do was to set the dial to the required number.

The librarians were two robots. They attended to anything that might. appear to go wrong. They could operate all the machines and trace any material within the library with ease and celerity. Once you mentioned the subject, title or author of your interest, the rest was easy for them.

Next we moved to the Confessional. A vast airless room that immediately struck one with panic. There was a row or chairs arranged in a horseshoe in the middle of the room. Satan informed us that this was the room in which the leaders of the various City States of Gehenna were disciplined. All those who in one way or another defaulted in their duties such as suppressing insurgencies or failing to awe their subordinates into servility. Once summoned to account for their activities, they would undergo despicable torture. Beating, electric shock, gas feeding, acid bath, fire or impalement into iron stakes.

The laboratory was even more horrendous. An abominable stench struck us as soon as the door opened. The smell of chemicals, blood and cadevers.

"Come right in, gentlemen," Satan encouraged.

"What a queer place?" Keega remarked.

It was a spacious hall with tables, benches, drawers and beds. There were shelves with glass doors full of bottles with labels. Test tubes. Jars. Tongs. Reference books. On the benches were beakers, flasks, distillers and plastic bags containing human waste. There were trays of human parts — bones, skulls, limbs and anatomical debris. On each bench were powerful microscopes and other equipment.

There were large deep freezers with sliding glass doors. Inside them lay cadevers, stinking of formaline. Their eyes popped out like marbles. All of them gave us the mischievous grins of the dead.

Satan informed us that here, dead souls could be reincarnated. They could be clothed in new physical forms. This depended considerably on their former lives, before they died. There was a machine called Soulpast, designed for this purpose. It released computerized details on the life the dead soul had led both on Earth and in Gehenna.

To demonstrate this, Satan pressed a switch. The figure that stared at us from the fluorescent metal plaque was familiar.

"It's Challenge," Keega and I exclaimed at the same time.

"Right." Satan conceded. "Now let's look at his life."

He pressed another switch. A slip of paper sprung out. He gave us the paper to read.

Name	:	Earnest Challenge Graves.
Nationality	:	American. New York City.
Born	:	1948
Died	:	1984
Occupation	:	Spiv. Mercenary Soldier.
Activities	:	Fought in Vietnam and Korea. Psychopath. Killed four boys and two girls. Sodomised the boys. Murdered three adults.
Earthly Death	:	Shot by police, resisting arrest.
Gehenna Death	:	Killed by an opponent in self-defence.
Next Life	:	Inquisitor in High Treason.

We looked at the paper, incredulous.

"Do you mean to say he will be promoted in his next life?"

"Not will be, my dear Kimuri," Satan corrected. "He already is. If one lives according to Satan's will both on Earth and here, he will always rise to greater ranks." He paused and gave us an enigmatic smile.

"Those who fail in one life are always given another chance. Finally if they fail in all, they may end up in Tophet where they are purged by fire devils, he said.

"Alas!" I cried out.

"What will happen to Major Gakuu?" Keega asked after a pause.

"Why?" Satan demanded.

"For killing Challenge."

"Nothing, really."

"But why, sir?" I joined in. "This is a murder case."

"Because, gentlemen, and you must understand, Major Gakuu only acted instrumentally to accomplish what was pre-ordained as the second fate for Challenge."

Keega and I exchanged furtive glances. Satan smiled.

"There are other departments where we have machines programmed to register and regulate natural phenomena like the changes in the weather in the entire Kingdom of Gehenna.

He paused to study our reaction.

"By releasing certain gases in the atmosphere the animals and vegetation could be drastically affected."

"How?" I enquired.

"Tremors of the earth, earthquakes, lightning, storms, eruptions of volcanoes and similar cataclysms would occur.

"How about amelioration of the weather?" Keega asked.

"Yeah, yeah. Even that," Satan answered. "Come, let me show you another section."

We were about to pass a door with an anvil reading 'VIGILANTE.'

"What is this?" Keega asked.

"This is the Security Department. We have a spire on top of the building. It collects information which is then computerized and registered here. There are several mighty robots. They attend to the machines and the Records Department. When there is something suspicious, they know what buttons, switches and keys to touch. There is a code language which only I can decipher. The alarm will reach wherever I might be."

"Then what do you do?" I asked, tentatively.

"Set Hell loose." Satan said confidently.

I did not understand. Yet if I pursued the subject he might become suspicious.

"How does the spire gather the information?" Keega enquired.

"In every direction in space there are monitoring satellites. They transmit the message. The spire acts as a sort of receiver. The process is, of course, more complicated than that."

"You have a very sophisticated method of keeping surveillance," Keega observed.

"Security is of vital importance," Satan said emphatically.

28

The next sign on the door read 'FUTURITY'. Satan slipped a switch. The door glided open. We stepped in. A huge machine which resembled a television set stood in the centre. Numerous knobs and switches lined the front.

"Using this machine, you can see through a vista of years into the future," Satan declared.

My head tingled with excitement. I could now understand why Satan was omnipresent, omniscient, and indisputable omnipotent.

"To be forewarned is to be fore-guarded." The old English adage could never be more applicable than in Satan's case. Is this why he often caught us off-guard? How proud he must be in his ultra modern world with all these strange and unique gadgetry!

I was tremendously impressed by his kinky, ingeneous and easy way of getting whatever he wished.

"I don't have to visit the various departments for information. I just press a button on this miniature computer in my belt. My watch, too, is another computer. Through them I'm able to communicate with the states. Each state has its own monitoring stations."

"Sir," Keega queried, "Can the machine also reveal what might happen to an individual from the present to the time of his death?"

"Precisely, yes."

"May I know what will happen on my impending trip to U.S.A., what kind of life I'll lead there and what my fate will be and where?"

Satan shook his head.

"Why not?" Keega implored.

"Because," Satan explained, "human beings could be very unhappy if granted the power to see into their future. They could be chronically disconcerted. Ignorance is the best cure in these matters."

"But still, sir, the future is there. Wouldn't we face it more boldly if we knew what to expect?" Keega persisted.

"No," Satan said with finality. "I demur. However, since you are so concerned, then know this: Each day you live has a lot to do with the future. What you do today contributes to tomorrow. Today binds yesterday with tomorrow. You can't hope to face the future when you want to escape your past. Come on, let's move on shall we?"

I saw my friend Keega was very dissatisfied. He abysmally failed to

29

hide his pique. As we moved out of the Futurity, the door smoothly closed behind us.

This was too much. We felt confused and disoriented. It would definitely take some time before all this jumble was sorted out in our minds. Probably once the experiences incubated, with time, they might reveal some hidden truths about Gehenna and the world we knew.

We passed through orphanages with various species of animals, birds, and insects.

"These are for study. The specialists dissect them to study their internal make up. This, in effect, enables them to carry out the multiplicity of tasks that I assign them."

"Who are these specialists, Sir?" I asked.

"They are experts in various fields. They include heart specialists, brain surgeons, bone specialists, pathologists, zoologists and psychiatrists."

After a pause he added, "They are also very adept at voodooism. They are capable of turning corpses into zombies, which are used in the police force and in the army."

Satan observed that we had seen enough to daze our minds. We returned for supper.

"The ladies will keep you company. Feel free. Enjoy yourselves. I'll see you again in the morning. So long," Satan said, rising from the Hot Seat, which suddenly receded below the floor of the parlour. A lid slid from one side of the opening and closed the hole.

"Thank you, sir, for everything," Keega said on behalf of both of us.

Before Satan left, he pressed a button on the floor. Then he vanished. The lighting in the room changed. Shadows frisked on the wall. Sound followed. We realized it was a film show.

A medley of perfumes wafted in to the parlour. The maids trooped in. They were all gorgeously dressed, as if they were going to attend the Mayor's Garden Party. Sparkling jewels, lipstick, polished nails and high heeled shoes. They curtsied to us by raising their legs in the air, then joined us on the couches.

Lubaina and Kamali served drinks all round. There was plenty to choose from. whisky, vermouth, spirits, beer, liqueur. We tasted all of them. I was particularly fascinated by the way the ladies gulped down tumbler after tumbler of liqueur. I was getting drunk. I tried a cigarette but

30

stumped it out when it made me feel sick. Gloria Gallows abruptly burst out laughing.

"Where are the saints who couldn't touch a drop last night?"

"Dead and buried," Keega joked. We all laughed.

Gloria lit a roll of opium. It's aroma filled the room.

"Try some," she said, offering Keega the stuff.

I was surprised to see Keega accept and essay the evil smelling stuff in his mouth. The ladies cheered him. They induced me, too, to try it. I felt myself rising above the ground with the couch and the room looking distorted.

"Kimuri," Keega called out, "Do you recognize the film?"

I didn't.

"It's *Nana*," Keega volunteered. "I've also read the book."

As Nana got more and more involved in seducing her wealthy lovers with her feminine charms, delaying tactics and ultimately leading them into her love nests to sate their fiery lusts, the women became excited and snuggled closer to us. They were already drunk. Keega and I were each flanked by two women, competing to win our attention.

Gloria proved the most extroverted of the four. She and Chattel Kamali were embroiled in an argument as to which of them had a right to Keega's favours. The altercation culminated in an exchange of blows. They scratched at each other in an attempt to disfigure one another. Clothes were torn into shreds.

"Put on the lights!" Keega shouted, while struggling to keep his furious women apart. No sooner had the lights come than the rivals charged at each other, both quivering with uncontrollable indignation.

"Hell hath no fury like a woman scorned," Keega remarked when I went to his aid in separating the pugnacious women.

"You leave them alone. They'll tire themselves," Trixy and Lubaina shouted with excitement.

"You, men. How can you spoil a good fight?" Lubaina reproved us drunkenly.

The rivals spat venom at each other. They rolled one another on the thick carpet. They scattered and broke things right and left.

The film was still running. Nana was singing to a big audience. But, then, one could not stay one's attention of the film.

"Are men twelve like the Apostles of Jesus?" Lubaina shouted above the din. "Why can't we follow the programme?"

"Shut up, you nymphomaniac!" countered Gloria, who now straddled Kamali, pummelling her on the head.

"Then please yourself, you lesbian," Lubaina retorted.

Trixy giggled happily. She grabbed me by the hand. I did not resist. There was a shuffling of feet behind us. I hastily looked over my shoulder, only to see Keega and Lubaina, hand in hand, running behind us.

Trixy was mad. Twice she inadvertently tossed me off the bed. Eventually, overly spent, I sank into a deep sleep; fatigue-dragged slumber.

CHAPTER FIVE

A novel spectacle greeted us when we emerged through the gate the following morning. At first we feared to approach it. We, in fact, decided to go back and report the matter to Satan. As we began to retreat, we heard frantic whistling. Major Gakuu beckoned us.

"Hi chums," he saluted when we joined him.

"Hi Major," Keega and I responded.

He already had a new denture. His wounds, too, had been rubbed with ointment.

"Never seen a machine like this before, hm?"

"Never," I replied.

"Hop in and let us get going."

He opened the door. We got in beside him. He started the engine by pressing a button. The machine glided forward. Shortly afterwards, clouds of dust and miasma were whirling behind us. We watched Gakuu curiously as he changed gears by touching different buttons.

"What a machine!" Keega exclaimed.

"Quite handy. Easy to operate too. All you need to do is to familiarize yourself with the right buttons for climbing hills, descending slopes, running on straight levels, acceleration, or when you want to fly over rivers and precipices."

"Do you mean it's capable of all those things?" I asked in disbelief.

"Oh, yes. And many more," Gakuu explained. "This screen here is known as 'photoscreen'. It focuses all that lies before you and brings it nearer. You could also use it for telephotography."

He pressed a button. On the screen we viewed the way ahead of us through the dense, dark forest.

Here and there, we observed various animals at rest, at play or munching their meals. At one point we saw two gigantic vampires with wings like those of a bat. They had sinister mouths at whose corners protruded long fangs.

"My!" Keega shrieked, "Can't we change the route?"

"Oh, but it's alright, Keega. We can cope with them," he assured us.

"See. You can take photographs through this screen. They are processed internally."

He pulled out pictures of the two vampires.

"Just like Satan's sophisticated paraphernalia," I ventured.

Gakuu nodded.

"It can also easily become camouflaged. When approaching danger, it gives out 'peril tones'. This switch here is for radio communication with my colleagues. The roof is adjustable. By pressing this button it parts in the middle and slides into the body. The body is bullet proof. At the front and rear are spotlights capable of emitting radio-active rays which could be used in case of intense danger."

"Then I'm sure it consumes a lot of gas," Keega surmised.

"No," Gakuu said. "It doesn't use such fuel."

"How?" I enquired.

"It uses electricity. The battery is very special. It produces the current on which the machine runs. The current is absorbed by a second battery which consumes it. When the first battery is exhausted, the process automatically reverses. This model of cruiser is known as the *Reality*."

"Who invented all these machines?" I wondered.

"We have all sorts of people from the world Herebefore. Engineers, mechanics, artists. People highly learned in all fields of human endeavours. The most successful among them are those who benefited the world with their unprecedented inventions during the renaissance."

I recalled what Satan had told us about the experts in Gehenna.

"Most of the inventions they had in mind but had no funds to finance or enough time to realize have been completed here. We surpass many extraterrestrial worlds in many spheres. We have the best architects, sculptors, actors and philosophers. Luckily for you, you are going to meet some of these wonderful people."

"Are you serious?" Keega asked with excitement.

"Yep."

"That will be great," I said.

"Good. Now, before I forget, I have some gifts for you."

We opened the packages which Major Gakuu proffered with eager anticipation. Like the cruiser, his gifts, too, were odd.

"This one," Gakuu pointed out, "is a camera. It is capable of taking photographs even in the dark. It requires no flashlights, no film plates. It contains special chemicals. Its coloured photographs are processed within."

"Just like the ones in the *Reality*?" Keega queried.

34

"Exactly," Gakuu conceded. "You turn this knob and the photographs emerge. See?"

"Yeah," we saw.

"Fine. Ever seen a watch like this one?"

Neither of us had.

"Very special, too." Gakuu demonstrated. "It gives you the precise time in Gehenna. Press the pinhead. The time is converted into Greenwich Mean Time — your Earthly time. It gives you the time in hours, minutes, seconds, degrees. The unique thing about it is that within it is enclosed a miniature camera, a radio, tape-recorder, television, compass and a calculator. They all work on an internal radio-active battery. You can use it for communication. Just like a police radio. You can also use it as a torch in the darkness. It emits peril tones when danger is imminent."

"We highly congratulate you," I rhapsodized.

"Oh, brother," Keega beamed and effusively shook Gakuu's hand. "Can't really say how grateful we are."

"I'm so glad that you appreciate them. I'm sure you'll find them very handy in an extremely daunting assignment awaiting us. But about that I'll tell you later."

Presently we reached the scene of Challenge's death. Vultures and sundry denizen soared all over the place. We watched with awe.

The *Reality* trundled along the bumpy track through the dense forest. Each time the cruise emitted peril tones we would hastily swivel our heads to see a beast menacingly advancing on us. Gakuu would light a repellant and the ungainly creature would scamper into the bush.

There were bands of chattering monkeys and baboons, who hurled fruits and branches of trees at us as we passed. Occasionally the whole forest reverberated with howling wind and the roaring of the animals. We were exceedingly excited to notice that our watches gave out peril tones at the same time as the *Reality*.

Sometimes the gigantic mountains towering over us burst open, disgorging lava and choking clouds of sulphurous smoke. But we were always prepared against the catastrophes. At other times it seemed as if our track was headed for a terminus. But, somehow, just as we approached, the apparent cul-de-sac would disappear and the road would zig-zag round the hills and continue.

We drove through marshes, then great plains with salty water pools.

We saw scrawny game, nibbling at dry tufts of grass. The numerous carcasses filled the air with abominable stench. Most of them had been picked clean by vultures.

Gradually as we approached Ahera village, the environment changed into a semi desert. Major Gakuu explained to us that this was the result of the wanton cutting down of trees, which had been going on for years. The trees had been used for timber, firewood and charcoal; yet no new ones were planted to replace those cut. The corrupt forest officials sold timber and used the money for their personal benefit. The herdsmen, too, followed with their undernourished livestock. They overgrazed, leaving the ground completely bare. Then strong winds blew the top soil off with all its humus. Whatever niggardly soil was left, was afterwards drained away by the rain into the rivers.

The inhabitants of Ahera, in their ignorance and sloth, did practically nothing to check this loss of soil. They cultivated on river banks. Others on barren rocky ground, whose yield was always poor. More often than not, it was stolen before it ripened enough for the poor gardener to harvest.

The cattle were scraggy and sometimes turned carnivorous. There had been occasions when they had mauled children and drunkards to death. They had a propensity for strong drinks such as *chang' aa* and *waragi*, which they frequently managed to unearth at the River Bank Distilleries.

Major Gakuu related all this to us as we travelled. Then finally we reached the straggling dirty village with all its conglomeration of pungent reeks; which gave the impression of being a vast dumping-ground of human wretches.

On garbage heaps one saw dead dogs, cats and occasionally a newly born baby or a premature decaying foetus. Children, goats, pigs, dogs, chickens and the aged foraged in this mess for any edibles.

The dogs were mangy. Others, deadly carriers of rabies. The goats were violent. Often they gored people to death. The pigs, too, were demonic.

Major Gakuu restrained us from spitting or tying our handkerchiefs around our noses and mouths to wad off the stench and aerial bacteria.

"It might offend them. Surely we don't want to be stoned to death?"

"No, please."

"Good. Then act just as if you were ordinary inhabitants of Ahera. Of course you look different but let's not attract too much attention. That's why we had to leave the *Reality* in the cave."

Their homes were built of practically any available materials: tin, packing crates, polythene paper, cartons, wood, tiles, mud and grass. We were amazed to see that in almost every corner we turned, there was an imposing church building, a gilt mosque or a temple.

"How come they have religious institutions here?" I asked Gakúu.

"There are people who feel that life can never be complete without the usual routine of partaking in one form or another of worship."

"Just routine?" Keega enquired.

"Yep. There are also those who can't exist without clinging to some mysterious power outside themselves. They, therefore attend the services to commune with their deities."

"But surely there must be people who are genuinely committed?" I ventured.

"Well, yes," Gakuu acquiesced. "But these are relatively few. Normally the aged and the simple. Mostly, the others have ulterior motives for attending."

"Such as ?" I pursued.

"To show off their modish clothes. To pass time. For entertainment. Young people even find romance there. Politicians use it as a political platform. Sometimes commerce flourishes there."

"How about their clergy?" Keega asked.

"Many of them are failed saints. They were priests on Earth. They revel in drunkenness and philandery. Among them are those who have insatiable lust for power and wealth."

"Do you mean that they have squabbles?" I asked.

"Oh, more than squabbles. Schisms. Sometimes rival factions fight. The splinter groups elect their own popes and bishops. In the case of Moslems there are self-styled Kadhis and Sheikhs."

"Do they believe in the doctrine of Heaven and Hell." Keega queried.

"Yes, they even predict the end of Hell. Limbo, Purgatory and all the other places shall unite with the living in celebrating their victory."

"Very interesting," I commented.

We passed dingy clubs and beer-halls crammed with boisterous multitudes. Outside, sitting on rocks, crates and forms were small groups of people with long straws huddled around a pot of opium. Amongst the throng were cantankerous, tattooed prostitutes, both male and female; their skins coated with heavy layers of cosmetics. They were all scantily dressed to display their wares.

Gakuu informed us that the majority of the patrons were men and women, strong enough to do meaningful work. They preferred to loiter, beg and rob.

Owing to the idleness of the residents of Ahera, any diversion was always welcome. A minor incident like a child fighting with another over food, or cocks feuding, pulled large crowds. Luckily for them, there was always something happening at one corner or another.

What really pricked our conscience was the sight of malnourished, sickly children and sinewy old men and women. It annoyed me exceedingly to note that the inhabitants of Ahera had neglected all the existing rules of health and hygiene, and were contented to wallow in this filthy sty of corruption, to their detriment.

We learned that most of the children left home as soon as they were weaned. The girls got jobs as ayahs and housemaids. They were normally underpaid, overworked and maltreated. As soon as they reached puberty, they plunged into prostitution.

The boys were employed as matatu touts, labourers, and apprentices for thieves and pickpockets. Most of the children we saw looked like little old men and women.

Ahera village often suffered catastrophes. Frequently, whole sections were gutted down by fires whose causes were always obscure. Children and livestock perished in these blazes.

An outbreak of plague had claimed three thousand lives. That was the only time the people had turned against rats. Despite the chief's warning, some people still ate rats. Then cholera followed and claimed its own toll. People had to learn the hard way the hazards that flies can wreak. The presence of the mosquitoes in the gutters and the dirty river that crossed the village had to stamp itself through epidemics of malaria and elephantiasis.

At certain strategic points, we observed crumbling shacks and hovels. These, with their miserable furniture, were meant to serve as schools. Most were run by missionaries and charitable organizations. The remaining few were government run. More often than not, the exercise was a farce. The teachers were constantly drunk and unkempt. The pupils found learning boring. They deserted and went out in search of mushrooms and termites

38

for food. Parents did not support schools. They just watched with detached amusement.

Hospitals were a sorry sight. We saw long queues with patients suffering from all imaginable diseases. The nurses were frustrated and rude. The doctors were unsympathetic and corrupt. They stole drugs. They only attended to patients who could pay for private treatment. The rest were kept waiting in the queues for days on end. There were cases of patients dying on the benches, unattended.

"My goodness!" I said in astonishment. "To survive here one would require a very high degree of longevity."

"Right," Keega supported. "Survival for the fittest."

"Yet, somehow, they manage," Major Gakuu replied. "Occasionally, people leave the village to smuggle drugs, liqueur, currency or foodstuffs. They return with money to spend."

"You mean they have all these things in these hovels?" I asked.

"Oh yes. You can buy almost anything here. T.V. sets, motor spare parts, jewels, guns, radios. They have their own doctors; most of them charlatans. Abortions are performed while you wait. You can also hire professional killers."

"The poor souls," Keega lamented.

"For your information, not everybody who lives here is poor. There are people who work in the city. This, to them, is a paradise where they obtain cheap accommodation, cheap beer and cheap sex. That's all they live for."

At one point, probably to assuage our passion for the suffering masses, our guide conjured up a poem:

> *Sympathy is a boon of weakness*
> *Be strong and betray no weakness*
> *If for yourself you fend*
> *You, then, have the might to defend*
> *Unless, of course, you're independent*
> *An' such orthodox course be repellent.*

All along, my friend Keega, the inveterate journalist, had been taking photographs and scribbling notes.

"Where is that groovy music coming from?" Keega queried as the sound of music drifted to our ears.

39

"It's a political rally," Major Gakuu answered. "The elections are approaching and politicians have returned to solicit for votes. Let's go and see."

CHAPTER SIX

The music turned chaotic as we got closer to the rostrum. There were several live bands with ultra modern guitars, organs and saxophones. They all seemed to be relentlessly competing with the church and school choirs and traditional dancers, all agog to glorify their candidates and benefactors.

Most people in the exuberant throng were drunk and rowdy. They all rancorously shouted different slogans and sometimes fought over their antagonism. They all wore tee-shirts over their rags. The shirts bore portraits of different candidates. Quite a good number were undernourished and barefoot. Nevertheless, everyone with a vote was important.

The police, assisted by the special units, plain clothes and party youth wingers moved amongst the multitudes with guns on which were borne bayonets and tear gas cannisters, to maintain law and order. The whole place teemed with spies.

Politicians, religious leaders and other dignitaries sat on the chairs on the rostrum. Some of them chatted, while others dourly smoked their pipes or fat cigars. There were several women candidates.

Up in the sky several helicopters flew low, tugging along fluttering pieces of cloth on which were inscriptions such as:

FOR PROGRESS AND PROSPERITY
VOTE FOR NYANG'AU

Another one read

NYOKA FOR EFFECTIVE REPRESENTATION.
YOUR PROBLEMS ARE MY PROBLEMS
VOTE WISELY: VOTE FOR NYOKA

Before the various candidates stood to solicit for votes, the area prefect appealed to the assembly to maintain peace and order so that the meeting should succeed. He swore that he would order the police to manhandle anyone who proved intolerable.

To our amazement, we could recognize several of the politicians. We had known them while they were still on Earth! We had seen the faces of others in newspapers and magazines. Some wore flowing West African garb, while others were in suits and carried fly-whisks on sceptres in their hands.

41

Major Gakuu gave us more information on the candidates. Among them were those who had built themselves up by embezzling public funds. Some had been directors of various co-operative or land buying firms. They misappropriated public funds and property. Consequently, they used their wealth to buy their way to power and prestige. Ndege and Kemeria were good examples.

There were others who had amassed wealth through smuggling and poaching. They crossed territorial boarders through their agents. They conducted market surveys. They ascertained what was in short-supply in neighbouring countries. They then sent lorry-loads of these commodities and sold them at outrageous prices. This, in effect, left their countries in want. Many families suffered lack of essential commodities. In some cases, these crooks were known to collude with senior police officers. Then they had their merchandise escorted by police vehicles.

Nyoka and Kamaliza had been charged with murder. Their cases were still pending. Nyoka, particularly, was notorious even back on Earth for murdering political and business rivals. He had at one time been held responsible for the deaths of hundreds of innocent school children.

Kamaliza was notorious for detention without trial of his political opponents. He had acquired enormous tracts of land for speculative purposes. He had built hovels of estates and apartments in all major towns. He charged exorbitant rents. With the accruing profits he had joined Mukarafuu. The two opened up private schools. They fleeced parents and pupils, providing them with substandard education. They grew wealthy. They joined politics.

Nyang'au, who bragged of being in politics longer than all the other candidates, had been a director of a fraudulent land buying company. Any members who brought up controversial issues regarding their money or division of their land disappeared mysteriously. He had also developed ways of evading or underpaying his taxes.

Two others; one a woman and the other a man, had been mayors. They had left their councils in financial mess. They still survived to contend for higher offices.

The candidates rose up one by one, each superciliously regaling the gathering with their advantages over their rivals. They harped at their achievements during their tenure of office. One of them even had the guts to claim that he was responsible for several projects which had been in the

42

government plan of the past decade. Another one tried to extenuate the absence of any development during his term in office by insinuating that, as a Senior Government Minister, he had been required to work outside the country and therefore found little time to be with his electors. The people unanimously resolved to cast no votes for him so that he would have all the time to serve the Government outside the country.

Gakuu informed us that some of the candidates were foreign sponsored. I wondered, inwardly, what kind of government such crooks could form and whether the same lot would fulminate against the very crimes they themselves had committed. I could not quite see any good reason why people would want to be in the same government that they had cheated. Or was this a facade to cover up their misdeeds? At any rate it is often said politics is a dirty game. And where could it be dirtier than in Gehenna!

One candidate, Taabu Leo, amused us immensely. When he was given the chance to talk he said:

"My people," he paused and looked around. He cleared his throat and continued. "I know you. You will not be happy with me if I tell you the truth. You have an affinity for falsehoods. You will only be pleased with me if I heap empty promises on you. You will be most happy with me if I make a mere display of my enormous wealth, even if it doesn't benefit you in any way. You will be happy with me if I keep you drunk and drugged. I may even feed you for a day and give you a tee-shirt. So far nobody has doled out trousers or dresses. But, my good people, all these things will not solve your problems."

"*Nyamaza*! Some of his fellow candidates rasped.

"*Toboa*! *Toboa*!" The crowd chanted.

"But if you don't vote for me this time," he paused and surveyed the throng. "If you don't vote for me this time, I will remember to use that formula during the next elections. You rejected me at the last elections because I had no wife. Now I have three."

There was rancorous laughter all around. Women ululated.

"Continue!" the crowd urged.

"For now we need people who will make the government aware of your problems. Even help you to find practical solutions. Tell me. Do we conserve energy to waste it on helicopters, running up there with ribbons the whole day?"

"Shut up!" Nyoka bellowed, menacingly.

43

"*Toboa*!" the crowd goaded.

"Are we of Ahera Village allergic to clean water? Look at you. Believe me, even pigs would feel ashamed of such habitation."

"*Kwenda*! You are insulting us!" Someone shouted.

"We need representatives that will bring education of Family Planning, nutrition and hygiene, and technical skills. We are all sickly, malnourished, jobless and homeless..."

"*Uuh*!" One of the women candidates screamed. "Traitor!"

The atmosphere was becoming tense. The prefect whispered something in Taabu Leo's ear. He nodded.

"Right. Just before I finish, listen. We need to think more seriously about our environment. You people need proper leadership. See. You have cut down all the trees. Now we have energy crises. No firewood. No charcoal. No oil. No timber. No rain. The desert is encroaching on us."

"Taabu *Juu*!" Shouted a supporter.

"*Kwenda wewe*, Taabu *chini*!" retorted a rival's supporter.

"Mmh." Taabu cleared his throat for attention. "How many schools do we have here?"

"You should know. You are a teacher," someone ejaculated.

"Fine. I'm a teacher. I'm your man. We need more schools than churches and mosques in Ahera. We need more health centres and improved health services. We need education for adults and less drinking of alcohol. Taabu Leo is your man. You forget that and you'll regret it before the next elections."

"Threats!" Nyang'au bullied.

"Detain him!" Kamaliza chimed in.

"*Uuh*!" a stentorian scream cut through the crowd, like a hot knife through butter. There was commotion all around. People pushed and jostled. Our watches gave out peril tones, frantically. Before we knew what was happening, Taabu Leo was hustled into a police van.

"What has he done?" I asked Gakuu.

"Inciting people and behaving in a manner likely to cause a breach of the peace."

"You mean truth is an anathema here?" Keega asked, shocked.

"Men," Gakuu parried, "this is Gehenna."

Suddenly I was hit on the head with a truncheon. I looked up only to see a legion of riot police surrounding us. People were shouting and running in all directions.

"Quick! Run! But don't run too far from me!" Gakuu bawled over the din. There was shooting and stone-throwing. More screams and stampeding. When we were a safe distance from the pandemonium, Major Gakuu said:

"That was hectic."

"Real hell, uh!" Keega observed.

"Hurry up," Gakuu prodded, "We have an important meeting this afternoon."

"Surely not like that one?" I objected.

"No, something more sensible than a political rally. Remember I warned you, we have an extremely difficult task ahead of us?"

"Yeah."

"Good. I also hinted to you about meeting those fabulous inventors and scientists?"

"Yeah."

"Excellent. That's the meeting."

"Okay, then," we acquiesced.

CHAPTER SEVEN

The conspiracy hatched in the 'void'. This was a vault in an old derelict church. The precincts were intensely guarded. They were fortified and surrounded with electric cables, electronic surveillance gadgets and ultra-violet cameras. Intrepid security guards stood at various strategic positions. Among the guards were robots and zombies who talked and behaved like human beings.

Before admittance, we were thoroughly screened. Details on personal dossier were confirmed. These precautions were in a bid to forestall infiltration and the possibility of anyone smuggling in dangerous weapons. Eventually, the Chief Security Officer ushered us in to the seats reserved for us.

The 'void' was jammed with people. Curious eyes peered at us anxiously. We were immensely abashed. For a while, we fidgeted and averted our eyes from those searing glares.

Major Gakuu gave us a reassuring smile. He helped us in adjusting the headphones connected to our seats.

The proceedings commenced immediately, with a brief introduction of the principal co-ordinators.

The mastermind was Professor Albino Wiseman. He was an invalid in a wheelchair, which, when connected to its other components, could serve as a single-passenger aircraft. We later learnt that he had a frail heart that only functioned with the aid of a battery-powered heart pacemaker. He was a dandy in an exquisitely cut three-piece suit, a fresh rose in the button-hole and gold chains on his waist-coat. He also wore a superlative gold-plated wrist watch and gold and diamond rings on his fingers. He was the esteemed holder of diverse science awards and a consultant for all leading universities in Gehenna.

Before him stood a large U-shaped table with piles of books, papers, charts, gadgets and a huge globe, illustrating the great amorphous Kingdom of Gehenna.

The Secretary-General was Doctor Reverend Felicitous Web. She was a parapsychologist, clairvoyant medium-cum-spiritualist. A tall imperious woman with mystic eyes. She retained her radiant youthful appearance through dieting, massage, vigorous exercises and plastic surgery. Her main task was to monitor, perceive and abate Satanic forces before they wrecked havoc against the meeting. She also had the power to heal all sorts of maladies, using supernatural means. Her magic wand lay on the table in front of her.

Mister Alexandrovitch Nikolai Brovsky was a tall gaunt scholar, clad in a sack suit. He was a specialist in geographics. He had been assiduously involved in designing and supervising the assembly of the majority of the equipment to be employed in the operation. He was an enigmatic fellow, with the raddled complexion of a drunkard. He seldom smiled.

Pope Innocent, who had acted as the spiritual adviser to the Syndicate, had been brutally murdered, just a few minutes before leaving 'Papalry', where the pontiff lived. His place had been instantly taken up by Cardinal Rob Driftsham I, who was present at the meeting. He was a stout man with chubby cheeks, shrewd green eyes and an effeminately shrill voice. He wore an enormous gold crucifix on the chest. His mouth was crammed with gold-teeth.

Keega and I were also introduced to the group. We were amazed at the amount of information about us known to the organization. We were immensely horrified to hear Major Gakuu introduced as Marshal Gikuu. Gikuu is the superlative of Gakuu. Both pertain to death.

The remaining set of people comprised men, women and children from all walks of life: doctors, military experts, religious leaders, legal specialists and students. They all had important roles to play. The entire organization was referred to as the Creation.

After the introductions, Professor Wiseman thanked all parties concerned for devoting themselves and their precious time to work through hard and strenuous conditions. He thanked the various political, religious and commercial organizations, as well as private individuals who had so generously contributed to this project.

It came to us as a profound shock that the Creation was formed with the express purpose of toppling Satan Lucifer; to capture and abduct him to the Earth to face trial before The World Court of Peace and Justice.

"Dear friends," Professor Wiseman began, "A comprehensive study by a team of experts has revealed that Satanic Powers are gaining a firm hold on Earth."

He regarded the audience to assess the impact of this news. A number of heads nodded.

"It is also clearly evident that if these powers are not duly curbed, they will produce very disastrous results. The Earth will be just a colony and a replica of Hell. Satan Lucifer and his ilk will ultimately have victory over God and His elect."

There were murmurs of exasperation in the 'void'. Suddenly I found myself flung into a state of disquietude.

"Comrades," Professor Wiseman continued, "this must be checked. It is utterly in opposition to God's plan in creation."

"Sure, sure" the audience agreed.

Professor Wiseman continued to narrate the sombre forebodings:

"Today, my dear friends, the world is threatened by Nuclear Arsenals. There is the looming danger of Bio-chemical bombs. Even small poor nations have found it fashionable to arm themselves to the teeth. This leaves the majority of their citizens starving.

"Added to these are natural catastrophes such as floods, droughts, famine, diseases, ignorance and poverty. Religion is losing its value to man. It has become politicised, commercialized, mystified and adulterated. Religious leaders are frequently immersed in the power-wrangles, fraud and immorality. Few people see the intense danger the Earth is in today as it turns more and more like Gehenna. We are all aware of the existing evils such as war, apartheid, sex discrimination and fanatical communalism, to mention only a few."

He paused and surveyed the throng.

"Brethren," he appealed, "we have a duty to step in before mankind destroys itself."

"What are we supposed to do?" Keega enquired, his voice hoarse.

"We must conquer Satan! We must subdue him. Topple him. Once apprehended, we shall extradite him back to Earth. A special court — The World Court of Peace and Justice — shall be set up to try his case. It's only with Satan's downfall that the dignity of man shall be restored. Mankind shall, once and for all, be emancipated from the nightmares of Hell. We shall not promise Utopia but at least we shall try to perpetuate love, peace, justice, equity and universal brotherhood of man. We shall guide the people to exterminate evil from their midst. To eschew it."

We listened to all this, dumbfounded. Did these people really know what they were up against or was this imbroglio of toppling Satan sheer rigmarole by a mentally deranged academic? I was assailed by an abyss of

48

despair; despair for the condition of the world, ground by forces of evil.

"Impossible!" I muttered inadvertently.

"Yes, Kimuri?" Professor Wiseman prodded.

"You people don't seem to realise how powerful Satan is."

All eyes were now focused on me.

"It's indeed possible, Kimuri," Professor Wiseman countered. "True, we shouldn't underrated Satan's power. A lot if money, precious man-hours, and manpower has gone into this project. I'm still sanguine of success if we all play our part with devotion and commitment. Remember, dear colleagues, sublime confidence is a pre-requisite to success."

"Have you considered the risks involved in this endeavour?" Keega queried.

"Yes. Certainly there will be death. There will be suffering. But, don't forget; nothing of lasting value can be achieved without sacrifice."

"True," Keega agreed.

"Gentlemen," Professor Wiseman continued, "You really do not know what Satan has in store for you. He can be devious and unpredictable. Besides the satisfaction of doing good for the benefit of mankind the success of 'Operation Satan' will also provide you with escape."

"Quite right, thanks."

I was impressed. Professor Wiseman seemed to have answers to every problem.

With the aid of a collapsible screen and a projector he proceeded to show us a film on Satan's domicile — the Mausoleum — and other vital installations. The film showed all the possible infiltration routes. The most conducive was through an underground tunnel that plunged right into Satan's ground.

Keega and I learnt we were supposed to serve as the internal link between the Mausoleum and the Creation. Trixy Waruo and Lubaina Zawadi Igbo would give all the necessary assistance. Both ladies were collaborators.

"Learn all that you can, within the minimum period of time," the professor directed. "A thorough knowledge of the terrain will be essential. Keep physically fit. This will help you build the necessary stamina and endurance to cope with any hardship. Be cautious! Our man should not have the least suspicion of what is brewing."

We nodded.

49

All members of the Creation took an oath of allegiance and secrecy. We swore to commit suicide rather than be caught alive. That way, nobody would be tortured into disclosing the working and the constitution of the Creation.

Keega and I were designated Senior Privates.

Marshal Gikuu was made responsible for all Creation affairs. No one had a right to interfere with his decisions.

Two spies who had attended the meeting posing as members of the Creation were forthwith ruthlessly put to death and incinerated.

Minister Brovsky inspected the Creation to ensure that the special combat uniforms which also served as communication media were in good working conditions. After this we were given details on sophisticated ballistic missiles and guns. These were not necessarily meant for fighting Satan, but to combat his juniors, who may resist and try to foil the coup.

Other clandestine meetings were scheduled to take place in different places. Marshal Gikuu would take us there.

We all shook hands. From then on, we used the term *Mundu* (man) as a kind of *pax vobiscum*.

* * *

The sky was on fire. The wind howled like a choir of demons. Thunder rumbled. Lighting lashed and the storm gathered.

We gazed at each other, baffled. Our consternation was heightened when we noticed the amazing transfiguration we had undergone. Our black hair and the beards Keega and I had affected had turned copper-red. Our otherwise dark-grey eyes had acquired a mysterious glint. Marshal Gikuu's appearance had become ostensibly cadaverous. His rasping voice sounded sepulchral. His artificial denture stuck out ominously.

Some distance behind us, we could see the fortified church, shrouded by a veil of mist. The tough looking guards scurried in different directions. Only the robots and zombies were left to cope with the emergency.

Presently, there was a loud explosion. The building was hurled into the air and scattered into debris. A gust of fire sent out billows of smoke, painting the fiery sky black.

"Now, what does all this mean?" I enquired of Gikuu, in a trembling voice.

50

"Nobody can quite conjecture the fickleness of Gehenna," he said enigmatically.

"What about this transfiguration?" Keega pursued.

"It's all part of it." Gikuu maintained.

"How shall we account for it, should Satan ask?"

"Well," Gikuu shrugged impatiently, "simply say you do not know. He should know better himself."

"I think so, Kimuri," Keega said doubtfully.

"At any rate what do we know?"

"Just one point, Private Kimuri and Keega. Remember you are now soldiers. It's against military laws to manifest cowardice the way you do. I could shoot you down!"

"My!" I gasped.

Gikuu had become callous, harsh and ruthless.

Keega and I exchanged furtive glances. We could see he meant what he said. I recalled how he had butchered Challenge. This was enough to give one nightmares.

"Good. Now let's try to get to the *Reality* before it gets too dark to find our way through Confusion Forest."

The circuitous route we had taken thrust us into the forest. Our fear mounted. We dreaded encounters with wild animals most.

To side-track our apprehension we discussed the political rally we had attended earlier on.

Taabu Leo had sounded a truthful and committed politician. But, just as he had observed himself, one who spoke the truth could not be very popular in a state dominated by corruption and falsehood.

Marshal Gikuu informed us of pestiferous governments led by sly men and women who perpetrated judicious murders in the name of justice and 'interests of state'. Leaders who were self-styled gods, with the temerity to do as they liked with human lives. Firing squads. Guillotines. Induced accidents.

He told us of lands with such rapid progress that the masses found it difficult to cope. This helped to give birth to more slums, smog and rubbish. Overcrowded cities with grandiose skyscrapers and unemployed, undernourished inhabitants. Prostitution and thuggery flourished. Things happened so fast that one could hardly distinguish between revolution and counter revolution. Every facet of society was adulterated in one way or another.

We were startled by a sudden rustling in the bush. We halted. A huge animal that resembled an elephant emerged. It blocked our way. Its body was completely covered with thick hair.

Keega and I shook with uncontrollable fear. Marshal Gikuu fumbled with his pocket. I expected him to pull out a gun. Instead, he pulled out a stick the size of a cigarette, which he lit. There was a peculiar smell in the air. As if suddenly gone berserk, the colossal animal scurried away from us; felling trees and combing bushes.

"What was that?" Private Keega asked.

"A mammoth," Marshal Gikuu replied. "It's in the elephant family. Mammoths are now extinct on Earth."

"Grace!" I intoned. "I never dreamt of seeing a pre-historic creature alive. I've only seen their pictures in books."

"You'll be surprised," Gikuu predicted, "You will see many more."

"What was the stick you lit?" Keega enquired.

"It's a repellent. Its odour is repugnant to most animals."

We encountered lions, tigers and apes, among other strange animals.
Suddenly, my friend Keega, screamed.

"*Uuuh*! we are finished!"

"Senior Private Keega!" Marshal Gikuu reprimanded. "Pull yourself together."

"Hell!" I cursed.

The eerie creature glared at us menacingly. It was like a nasty bag of bones. The massive, powerful tail lashed from side to side, trying to reach for us. Its throat moved up and down spasmodically.

Gikuu shot at it as it started advancing towards us. It fled into the shrub.

"What a queer creature!" I ejaculated.

"Yep," Gikuu rejoined. "Would you believe that it is capable of climbing trees?"

"What ?" Keega and I chorused, astonished.

"On yes," Gikuu smiled sagaciously, "It is as good on land as in the forest. A competent swimmer in the water. Ruthless, too."

"*Andu* (men)" I urged , probably prompted by intuition, "Let's make haste and get away from here."

Just then, we saw it. A sinister monster glowering at us with mesmerizing red eyes. Its white body was covered with a fluffy coat of fur. It had a copious mouth with broad bloody lips. Yellowish, crooked fangs protruded at the corners. The muscular arms with long claws were set to tear us apart. The beast was over twelve feet tall.

"*Uuh!*" we screamed. "Help!"

"Shut up, fools," Gikuu commanded peremptorily. "You'll attract others by your cowardly screams."

"What shall we do then?" Keega snivelled.

"Sober up! Control your fear, behave as befits soldiers!"

The ghoul advanced on us. We retreated, terrified.

Gikuu fired. The bullet hit the target on the right shoulder. It did not fall. There was only the smell of burning fur. Now, more incensed, the monster set on its attack, more resolutely.

"Fire again!" I urged, animated.

My heart was in my mouth. My feet felt weak. No! I told myself. I won't let the shock overwhelm me.

"Please, Satan, spare our lives for once," Senior Private Keega prayed.

"It's a ghoul. Keep moving backwards and run when you can. Be careful you might get lost in the forest. Once again, don't run far from me. Do you hear me, men?"

"Yes, sir," We replied hopefully.

He shot again. Again. Again and again. The monster let out an ear-shuttering howl. Then in the distance we saw clouds of dust.

"Dooms-day!" Marshal Gikuu swore. "The others are coming to its aid. If only we could get to the *Reality*!"

The dauntless ghoul still pursued us, dragging its heavy fury legs. Gikuu flushed his lighter. He lit a thick dry bush. Smoke rose, spreading in curly wisps to the heavens. The bush crackled triumphantly. Birds from the neighbouring trees shrieked out warning in flight.

We managed to cover a considerable distance before the leading ghoul could skirt the inferno. There was a cacophony of confused noises from the frightened animals in the forest. At times, we collided with rhinoceroses. Elephants and huge forest snakes, with their venomous tongues emitting a spectrum of colours. ,

The *Reality*, we hoped, would not be too far. Our speed, however, was drastically hampered by protuberant roots that caught us unawares and

53

sprained our ankles or sent us sprawling to the ground. We gasped for breath. We felt utterly exhausted. Yet the weird noises from the ghouls persisted.

Marshal Gikuu led the way. Senior Private Keega followed. It was sheer torture striving to keep in pace with them.

"Come on, officers," Marshal Gikuu prodded, "Put in more effort. We shouldn't have far to go now."

We paused and listened. Silence.

"We've lost them," Keega remarked hopefully.

Hope can be soothing at times, especially in very desperate situations. I thought I was beginning to understand why people trusted so much in hope. But, even then, do not millions of people die hoping?

Soon, we noticed something frightful close by. Stalking and dogging us was a gigantic white body.

"Look out!" I yelled.

We bolted, again. The woods were gradually clearing. Gikuu shot at them again, to confuse them. This gave us sufficient time to reach the *Reality*. We scrambled on the seats without opening the doors. By this time the leading ghoul was only ten meters away.

"Drive off, sir," I hollered.

"What are you waiting for?" Keega demanded.

"Relax, men. Take your time, study them. You can even take pictures if you like," Gikuu offered aplombly.

"Gosh! What good will that do when we are perishing?" I shouted back at him, smouldering with rage.

Keega impetuously bent forward to press a button. Gikuu restrained him.

"Don't," he said placidly, "You'd only ruin the game."

The ghouls approached. When they noticed we were no longer fleeing, they hesitated. They emitted neighing laughter. Then they advanced on us threateningly, jabbering and grunting.

"Are you mad, Gikuu?" I shouted at him in exasperation.

"Hope, please," he replied sardonically.

"I tell you, Kimuri, they're in league to kill us. Believe me, brother. Now we're finished," Keega accused.

By now the belligerent ghouls were contriving their line of attack. They surrounded us on all sides. Marshal Gikuu pressed a button. The

54

Reality did not move. Our fear intensified. I was about to scream for help when the vehicle suddenly jerked, then as if elevated by an automatic jack rose up in the air. Gikuu ignored our frightened chatter and stream of curses, and concentrated on the buttons. The *Reality* started to revolve, slowly at first, then gained speed."

"It's not moving," I announced.

"Come on, Kimuri, Let's jump off and run for our lives."

"Nonsense," Marshal Gikuu snarled in his sepulchral voice. His face indicated clearly he could brook no more nonsense.

Then it happened. From the front of the *Reality*, a pencil of light fell on the confused creatures. They howled deplorably, in agitation. One by one, they began to fall, lifting their massive arms to their faces in an endeavour to shield off the light beams.

When they realized their number was dwindling, the survivors retreated in discomfiture, crying in anguish. They disappeared into the forest.

"Haven't you jumped off yet?" Gikuu scoffed.

We looked away in shame.

"You may hop down now, gallant soldiers, and view your slain enemies," he directed. "They're all dead."

We studied the ghouls. Their white fur was beautiful and soft. Sometimes it is astonishing how attractive dead things can seem. Their claws were hard. The fangs were strong enough to crunch a human knee bone. The females were slightly smaller than males. They bore two firm breasts on the chest.

"What do they feed on?" I enquired.

"Meat, fruits, vegetables and blood," Gikuu informed us. "They are very clean creatures. Sometimes you can find them at the river, bathing. Just like humans. Let's get going."

We got back into our vehicle. Gikuu pressed a button to lower it to the ground. Within no time, we were cruising through the jungle. He dropped us at the spot where he had picked us in the morning. We saluted and watched until he faded in the distance. Then we started walking to the Mausoleum, where Satan Lucifer was waiting for us.

CHAPTER EIGHT

The grand Mausoleum blazed in front of us in psychedelic colours. Frantic music filled the air. A melange of fragrance from flowers, incense and perfume diffused the atmosphere. Birds twittered gaily in the twilight.

Satan Lucifer, tall, strong and distinguished, was leaning on the balustrade of the balcony of the seventh floor.

He flashed us a most disarming smile. His manner was ostentatiously charming.

"Here you come at last!" he called out in a jovial lilting tone. We levitated to join him on the balcony.

"Did you have a good time?" he asked, regarding each of us in turn.

"Yes, sir," Keega replied, "Splendid. We even had some adventures with the police and some sinister monsters."

"What happened?" he enquired, interested.

We narrated our escapades.

"Mmh," he beamed. "I see you have even acquired a beautiful tan on your skins. Your hair is exotic."

Keega and I glanced at each other, perplexed. How could we account for this transmogrification?

"Yes, thank you, sir," I said, still bewildered.

"Let's go in to supper."

As we followed him into the parlour, we admired his magnificent dark brown robe. It was emblazoned with currency from different countries on Earth in various denominations; the US dollar, the German Deutschmark, Sterling Pounds, Kenyan Hundred Shillings note, Kwachas. The robe was exquisitely festooned with gold buttons.

The furniture had been changed. Everything in the parlour was dazzling.

After the ambrosia, the maids in gorgeous apparels and sparkling jewellery, cleared the table and served drinks. There was plenty to choose from: gin, beer, wine, whisky and liqueur. We settled down to a convivial evening.

In the course of our conversation, we learnt a number if things from our flamboyant host.

"Sir," I ventured, "back on Earth people talk of Satan being a frightening, grotesque monster. An apparition too dreadful to meet. Are you the same Satan or should we construe these allegations as mere fantasy?"

"Well, my dear Kimuri," Satan chuckled sweetly, "There are too many stories pertaining to my nature, character and appearance. Certainly you've seen pictures portraying me black. I've also been assumed to bear other forms: a woman, a serpent, warewolf or any other terrible spectre one could conceive."

"That's what brings about the confusion," I pointed out.

"Right," Satan conceded. "The fact, however, is that it is within my power and choice to exist as I like."

We stared at him in amazement.

"I can even exist in an invisible form. You wouldn't, for instance, believe that I was present at your arrival in Gehenna."

"Were you?" Keega and I asked simultaneously.

I recalled that mysterious presence as we blundered through the cemeteries, through the Evil Forest, then the voice droning a poem on death. The erratic skeleton that had oddly acquired flesh to become our debonair host. Now I could put the pieces together. They made sense. The prince of darkness, too, had his powers.

"Oh yes, Satan continued, "Of course you hadn't seen me. Not until I revealed myself to you. I reversed the normal process of death where a person dies, rots and is ultimately, reduced into nothing but bones." He permitted a wry smile.

Keega and I gaped at each other in utter incredulity. We had not imagined the process was reversible. Was this not a chemical process, hence irreversible?

"What happened to the other skeletons?" Keega enquired.

"There weren't any other skeletons," Satan laughed mirthfully. "What you thought were other skeletons was a hypnotic product of your fear."

"Sir," Keega said gingerly, "You have just admitted that what human beings say about you is not entirely wrong."

"Yeah."

"How did they come to know about you unless you revealed yourself to them as you're doing to us?"

"Fine," Satan replied, "It's quite true that you are not the first persons to visit Gehenna."

We listened avidly.

"Others came, especially in medieval ages of the Church. Some were ambitious enough to sign pacts with us. To have all their Earthly delectations gratified. Then after death they would relinquish their souls to me."

"What happened?" We pressed.

"Human beings are fickle. In their greed they were myopic. When they approached their death, all of them wanted to have their souls. They forgot that you cannot eat your cake and have it. They ended up here." He paused to laugh triumphantly.

"Some turned fanatically religious. They strived to warn their counterparts. They told them all that they knew about Gehenna and its sovereign, but all in vain."

I lit myself the eighth cigarette since the interview started. I inhaled deeply, then released the smoke in a thin jet. I watched it as it curled upwards, free and untrammeled towards the open windows.

"I see, Kimuri, you are wondering about the cemeteries."

"Yes, sir," I said in astonishment. "How did you know?"

"I see you are surprised," he laughed superciliously. "By now you ought to have realised that I have the power to read the mind. I can even direct what it should think and dictate the action it should take. This is how I induce people to do things they wouldn't do of their own accord, even the clergy and their faithfuls. I catch them unawares. They do my will," he laughed happily.

We watched him in startled bewilderment.

"The cemeteries?"

"The cemeteries serve as our sovereign emblem. I'm sure you must also have heard the cacophony heralded by a strong wind. Lightning and the rumbling of thunder, after seeing the cemeteries. That is our Supreme Anthem. When it plays, strict attention should be paid to it, either voluntarily or involuntarily. That's why you were momentarily transfixed."

We turned all that he told us over in our minds trying to make sense out of it.

"Come on, men," Satan said rising up, "You need to relax and have some fun in the hall."

The phantom Hall was one of the wings of the mausoleum. It was niftily

58

and extravagantly furnished.

The immediate attraction was the music machine. It continuously eddied vivacious melodies, one after the other.

On the glamorous walls neon lights flashed. Fantasy. Illusions. Mirage. Falsity. Phoney. Phantasmagoria.

As my eyes roved round the hall taking in the brilliant aromatic flowers and paintings by master artists of all ages, I spotted something that made my breathe catch in my throat.

Keega followed my gaze.

At one corner, near a drinks cabinet stood two waxworks, perfect facsimiles of Keega and I. They were dressed in the begrimed rags we had had on the night we arrived in Gehenna. The one representing me even had a bandage on the leg.

Satan seemed amused by our bemused reaction.

"Very refined art, isn't it?" he asked, laughing jestingly.

We were further embarrassed when the maids joined in the laughing.

"Relax, men," he said commiseratingly.

Trixy Waruo offered me a brandy. Kamali did the same for Keega.

The maids demonstrated magic shows and dances.

Lubaina Zawadi, for instance, killed Chattel Kamali. We witnessed that she was really dead. No breathing. No pulses. No batting of an eye lid. The body cold and stiff. Then, appealing to Legba, the god of voodoo, she resurrected her.

We were stuned.

By consulting the dginn, Scubian and Scubbi, she gave us accurate information about our backgrounds. Our fears, hopes and aspirations. While doing this she trembled like one possessed.

Trixy Waruo rose up to recite two romantic poems. As she stood there in front of us talking in a well modulated voice, I could hardly conceal my admiration for her puerile beauty. I felt that I was inordinately falling in love with her.

When she finished, she came and sat next to me.

"That was a swell performance," I complimented her.

"Thanks."

"Were they original?"

"Sure."

"Great."

I rose up and staggered over to study the music machine closely. Gloria Gallows playfully intercepted me and we started dancing to the waltz. She pressed herself against me and fondled me salaciously.

Satan smiled encouragingly.

I paid her perfunctory compliments about her tattooed body and scanty attire. She giggled sexily into my ear:

"I hate you" she whispered.

"But why?" I asked amazed.

Amused by the perplexity, she led me to the drinks cabinet and mixed cocktail for both of us.

"Now, fellows," Satan announced, "I'll leave you to your own devices. Feel free. Relax. Dance. Drink and make love. All to your predilection."

He smiled broadly.

"For any song you want just shout to the 'music machine'. If you'd like to know the appearance of the artistes – dead or alive – watch the screen. They will demonstrate, just in case you're not familiar with some of their styles."

Once again we marvelled at the wonders of Gehenna. Satan Lucifer seemed to have an ingenious and kinky way of getting anything he fancied.

"If hell can be this enchanting, I wonder, then how beautiful Heaven is," I observed.

"Upon my word," Keega interjected, "Heaven is full of thorns and rough roads, tribulations and persecutions. The gates are so narrow that you would have to strive to enter. At least so we were told by a priest in a Sunday School class."

"I remember hearing the same thing myself," I retorted, "Only this time it was from a Sunday School teacher and not from a priest."

"To me they're all the same, anyway." Keega rejoined.

One would shout a special request as soon as one song was over. If more than one song was called for, they played consecutively. All the songs were popular. Love songs. Hate songs. Nonsense songs. Elegies. Dirges. Marital music.

Suddenly, I noticed that Trixy and Lubaina were no longer with us.

"Where are Waruo and Zawadi?" I enquired.

"Probably they have gone to powder their noses," Keega suggested.

We drank. Danced. Made love.

Kamali and Keega smoked opium from a pot.

"*Mundu*!" I warned, "You'll go mad."

"Keep on talking, buddy. When you're done with, you might as well light yours and try. It's good."

"You try," Gloria nagged.

I did. I felt myself transported into realms hitherto unexplored. I felt happy. Ecstatic!

"You know what, fellas?" I enjoyed making noise. "I'm and African hippy, yeah!"

"Yeah! Yeah! Yeah!" the others chorused.

"Lets have more music!" I yelled.

"That's 'Fra Divolo'," Gloriah said, linking her hand with mine.

"What's that?"

"Means Brother Devil," she said. "It's swell, isn't it?"

"I guess so."

Hand in hand we lumbered over to a couch at the far end of the hall. We snuggled close to each other and kissed. Her lips were tender, sweet and trembled with lust.

"Now look at those two," I whispered propping her head so that she could see Keega and Kamali madly fumbling with each other.

"I love you, G.G.," I mumbled kissing her on the neck.

"Nonsense," she parried, pulling me towards her. "It doesn't work."

"What?"

"I hate you."

"Mmmh?" My lips were burning. "What have you done to me?"

"Phitre."

"Love portion. I mixed it with your drink. You can't resist me anymore, Kimuri."

When Trixy Waruo and Lubaina Zawadi returned, we were playing cards and debating heatedly. Gloria had raised the motion that "All women are whores."

I proposed the motion.

"Women have made efforts to attract man's attention throughout the ages. Isn't it the same thing that drives them to use cosmetics, beauty saloons, massage parlours, plastic surgery, pills and to change from one fashion of dress to another? If men do not seem to notice this and compliment them, they'll sob themselves blind and let Hell loose."

61

"Yeah," Keega prompted.

"Then there is the question of the woman's readiness to abnegate herself totally and sacrifice herself, body and mind, to a man because of his property, fame, political or social status."

"Is that all?" Keega taunted, swirling his liqueur in his goblet, reflectively.

"Add to all these the fact that she has to demand alimony when divorced," Gloria contributed.

"Exactly," I agreed.

"Just a moment," Keega said pointing an accusing finger at me. "If I get you right, you are suggesting that even marriage is another form of prostitution, right?"

"In a way," Gloria answered, nodding her head and blowing breath on her knuckles.

"In communities where men accept dowry and inheritance from women, say like English, Russian, Asian and certain African peoples, would you offer this as prostitution?"

"No, not really," I hastened to argue.

"Two. In the mordern world, there are men who'll marry a woman for property, her job or wealth. Would you consider such men whores?"

"Certainly, you would," Kamali piped in gleefully.

"Three, we may define a prostitute as a woman who relegates her body for sexual pleasure to a man who will pay her in money, gifts or otherwise, prior or after copulation. Tell us why the same term should not apply equally to a man who accept payment from old women, invalids, divorcees, widows and nymphomaniacs to quench their lust?"

The debate was becoming hot. Trixy Waruo, at this juncture, pulled me by the hand and led me to the couch on which I had made love to Gloria. She briefed me on all that had transpired during their absence from the party. Marshal Gikuu, wearing the face of Death, had paid a reconnaissance visit to the Mausoleum. The two maids had taken him around. He had inspected the installations and the security systems. Before his departure, he had expressed his despondency over our participation in 'Operation Satan.' He had decried our over indulgence in alcohol, sex and drugs.

We returned to find Kamali whirling round and round, spilling liqueur on her dress.

"Cheers," she shouted for joy. "Men are little children! Dependent on

62

women. Helpless bastards!"

"I think we're getting too high to keep our heads level." Keega said emerging from another corner with Zawadi.

In bewilderment, we watched Gloria and Kamali kissing each other, passionately. So Trixy was right when she had called her a lesbian!

"Reverend Keega, oh yeah!" I said, rising to go to sleep.

"Oh yeah!!" the others rhapsodized drunkenly.

We all rose and kissed each other good night. As we tottered along, Senior Private Keega began a song:

> *I'm a soldier In the Army*
> *I'm a soldier In the Army*
> *I'm a soldier In the Army*
> *If I die let me die, in the Army*
> *If I die let me die, in the Army*
> *If I die let me die, in the Army*
> *I'm a soldier In the Army of the Lord*
> *I'm a soldier In the Army of the Lord*

We all joined in raucous voices. Near our bedrooms I heard myself inadvertently shouting:

"All women are whores!"

"All men are slaves!" back came the recrimination from the resourceful Gloria Gallows.

We all burst into boisterous laughter. We had not thought of that. Probably next time we shall debate whether "All men are slaves."

At the door, we parted with the dictum:

"Life is what you make it. See you when you see me. *Bonne nuit.*"

CHAPTER NINE

The Airship was called *Life*. It resembled a weird giant insect. It did not require any runway. It could simply spring up into the air with a single leap, after the pilot pressed a button. It had a snub-nose and a box fuselage. On each side were short delta wings which, like its spindly legs, could also be folded back into the sockets. They aided its manoeuvres in space.

There was a barograph which recorded altitudes as we rose up and down in the air. unlike the noisy Earthly aeroplanes, here one did not require earphones. There were no ear-shattering motors.

Like the *Reality*, *Life*, too, generated its own energy which circuitted through a convulated system before being absorbed and conserved in a separate battery. When one became exhausted, the other one automatically functioned.

The panchromatic camera at the bossom of the *Life* took coloured photographs. These were instantly processed and printed by a computer.

On approaching danger, the aircraft emitted peril tones just like the *Reality* and our unique watches. The object of danger would then presently be reflected on the 'photoscreen'. The body of the *Life* was all bullet and gas proof. Capable if releasing radio active rays. There was also a special oxygen reserve system.

Flying in the *Life* was an intriguing sensation. It ascended majestically in space. The landscape below seemed to recede beneath.

The Mausoleum, the vegetation and the mountain ranges started diminishing as we rose higher and higher. We experienced a magnificent euphoria of weightlessness, akin to the one we felt while levitating.

"Look! What's happening?" Keega shrilled.

We hastily gazed down.

On one of the hills below, rocks were being thrust violently in all directions. Then the ground burst.

"Extruding lava," I observed.

"Right. They're quite common here," Gikuu informed us.

Without any warning at all, an erratic gale blew, vociferously. Thunder crashed. The ground trembled. Eerie noises filled the air. Invisible owls hooted sporadically.

"We're in Demonland," Marshal Gikuu announced.

"Seems a very queer place," Keega said.

"Inhibited by all sorts of malign spirits. If you happen to pass here by night, you see dark, shaggy spectres performing all sorts of orgies."

Next came the Cannibia. A vast territory inhibited by cannibals who thrived on human flesh and blood. Peering down from the air we could see hordes of them collected round bonfires, relishing human delicacies. They exhibited diabolic exultation in this lunatic holocaust.

Their chief victims were a simple community of proletarians and peasants, serfs and slaves who dwelt in their neighbourhood. Without these unfortunate folks whom they lured on to destruction with food and other valuables like money and ornaments, their existence would be doomed.

We had little difficulty in crossing through warring territories. We learnt from Marshal Gikuu that most of the rowing, feuding and massacres was a result of disrespect for the boundaries of neighbouring sovereign states, or interference in their internal affairs.

Some states were embroiled in wars of independence from imperialist oppression and exploitation. Almost invariably, the oppressors happened to be the minority. Their strength, though, lay in support of their brothers elsewhere and their logistic superiority.

Others were independent states arrogating themselves all those fashionable qualifiers like "Democratic Republic...", "Democratic Federation of....States." These were steeped in civil wars owing to nebulous or petty causes springing from selfishness, desire for self-aggrandizement through tribal sanctions, sectionalism, or racism. Religion, too, served as a disruptive factor. All this was done purpotedly, in the name of peace, justice, freedom, security, unity, progress and umpteen other reasons. Others even revelled in military take-overs.

In most cases, we observed, there were superpowers, or sponsors, who armed the rival states to the teeth with the most sophisticated and newly invented armaments to annihilate their starving brethren. At any rate, they had to fetch markets for their industrial products which included nuclear weapons. At the same time, they got employment for the surplus population as mercenaries. The best way to achieve these ends and to provoke their fellow competitors in the arms' race was to declare spheres of influence on poorer states.

We observed ruins of civilization. The devastating effects of the neutron bomb. Buildings left intact in unpeopled ultra-modern cities. Mass suicide?

In other areas we saw ghostly-thin soldiers, keeping guard over scraggy, unkept prisoners of war, hostages, fugitives or political dissidents.

Elsewhere, vultures soared all over battlefields, feeding on the carrion which littered the place. Hyenas laughed with contentment. Ironically, they were often better fed, and thus, fatter than their benefactors.

In another place, some soldiers and guerillas, silhouetted against trees, tried to shoot us down. *Life* proved tough. Their bullets boomeranged. Then by becoming camouflaged, the *Life* would fly higher, above the lurid clouds.

Detention, intern and rehabilitation camps, like prisons, barracks, and homes for the aged and the destitutes, were in atrociously appalling conditions. Unutterable brutality went on there. Torture, cold-blooded murder, rape and mutilation. Captives were whipped, hammered, or clubbed to death. Their carcases were fed to crocodiles, sharks and scorpions in ponds or other hungry beasts in dens.

Even those countries which had ceased fighting were fraught with new problems; famine, inadequate medical supplies and shortage of essential commodities. The requisite foreign exchange for commercial intercourse became scarce. Diplomatic relations, in most cases were strained or severed altogether.

Furthermore, natural catastrophes such as floods, devastating droughts and pestilence followed. These were occasionally escorted by scourges of locusts, lemmings and army worms. Such a situation exposed a country to the mercy of any willing donors. Where the conditions proved unbearable, they accepted aid, even with strings attached.

The *Life* began transmitting peril tones. The photoscreen indicated jet bombers approaching at the speed of light.

Keega and I were flustered. Marshal Gikuu remained calm and composed.

"Here, commandos," he called out in a voice completely free of emotion. "Be ready for fun. You watch the screen, I'll attend to them."

It was short. it was quick. And, indeed, fun.

From the photoscreen we could discern the *Life* gain speed, as if in endeavour to shake off the high-powered fighters. They began to shoot. A hail of bullets aimed at our craft. They deflected before hitting us, falling to the ground. The air-force boys were excited. They entered into bitter recrimination against each other. Some feigned mechanical defects and retreated. Others tried to surround us from all sides. The atmosphere reverberated with engine noise and explosions. They closed in on us. That is when it happened.

Marshal Gikuu jabbed a button. The surface of the *Life* was outlined against a brilliant pulsating white glow that dazzled our assailants, sending them hurtling down. They burst into flames. We sighed with relief.

"I thought we were finished!" I remarked.

"Cowardice and adventure don't go together," Gikuu rejoined. "I thought by now you were already inured against the conditions of life in Gehenna."

"But nothing is ever the same here," I countered.

"The only thing that is certainly constant in life is change," Gikuu returned.

"Your argument reminds me of a poem I composed in bed this morning," Keega said.

"How does it go?" Gikuu asked with interest.

Keega recited:

> *Life is full of surprises*
> *Each day carries its own*
> *Some for better, some for worse*
> *Though seldom revealed by dawn*
> *It's we who always pay the prices*
> *But all with time may come to pass*

"Excellent! Such is life," Gikuu commented. "Ever so erratic. Here they come again with reinforcement, to give us more fun."

There was sudden pandemonium as jet fighters charged, spewing a cavalcade of missile, which again deflected before hitting the *Life*. After beguiling them that they were actually subduing us, Gikuu pressed a button. An avalanche of gamma rays immediately set the bombers ablaze, shattering them into pieces

"That should teach the fools not to interfere with us next time," Gikuu said triumphantly.

Shamblesville. A confluence of vanity in all its multiple dimensions. It resembled one of the earthly cosmopolitan cities; New York, London, Moscow, Paris, Peking, Tokyo, Lagos, Karachi or Nairobi. The city sprawled out like a carpet daubed with a pattern of houses, parks and gardens.

From the side which we entered the city, one felt almost certain one were moving over the intrinsically clean streets of Singapore. There were police officers in clean uniforms patrolling the area. Marshal Gikuu informed us that this was the residential area for the aristocrats, the billionaires, millionaires, counts and lords. Among them were the leading transport magnates, oil and rubber barons, bankers and financial experts.

This privileged cream of the society lived in constant fear and suspicion of their wives, vicious mistresses, children and servants. Many of them, in spite of their affluence were constantly haunted by thoughts of kidnap, assassination and blackmail. Moreover, they dreaded the thought of being robbed and reduced to common men.

The barricaded homes of the rich were under perpetual surveillance by police, detectives, guards and fierce dogs. Here, one saw the best bungalows, mansions flatlets and an occasional castle. The residents used first class means of transport.

Past this exclusive residential area, we came across a number of government offices affiliated to various ministries.

The Ministry of Madness and Personal Convictions dealt with matters of principle, conscience, physical and metaphysical issues. The secretary and his assistants were versatile philosophers. Some of them were staunch disciples of Plato, Aristotle, Confuscius, Karl Marx, Engels and Lenin. The Ministry of Information dealt with facile propagation of scandals, libel, gruesome news, lies, general misinformation and commercial advertisements. The Ministry of Tourism and Prostitution ensured that there were posh hotels where tourists could, with all due privacy, carry out their nefarious activities, which included sexual orgies. Some of them experimented with sowing new disease bugs into their unsuspecting money-hungry victims. Some of these diseases proved incurable and expensive. Tourists with lust for violence, too, satiated their sadistic perversions. They murdered.

Among the tourist too, were often criminals on the run and those particularly interested in cultural pollution.

68

The Ministry of Economy was charged with the task of raising revenue. This sometimes resulted in the exploitation of the poor by government officials, over-taxation and ever spiralling cost of living. There were, allegedly, many cases of embezzlement of funds for development projects. Consequently, the rate-payers were constrained to tighten their belts: to contribute to fill the deficits.

The Ministry of Justice and Social Order was riddled with corruption and malpractices, such as graft, bribery, tribalism and general chaos.

Most courts were notorious for losing evidence especially in the form of court exhibits from criminal investigation files. It was not unusual for officials to lose exhibits, even as significant as cars, aeroplanes, corpses and murder weapons. Cases were known when murderers were released for lack of sufficient evidence to convict them though they were guilty.

In other instances, suspects stayed long in remand while their cases were under investigation. At times, after languishing in jail for years, it would come to light that the convicted had been mistaken for different people. Others were discovered innocent after completing jail terms or while serving their jail terms.

Policemen often turned into thieves and robbed the people they were supposed to protect.

Other ministries we came across included: The Ministry of War and Peace, the Ministry of Education and Conditioning, the Ministry of External Affairs, dealing with all exterritorial matters, including ambassadorial duties in Gehenna, Earth and elsewhere.

The city was a forum of pollution. There were diverse construction works in progress. One's nerves were jarred by interminable noise from trucks, cranes, the roaring of bulldozers hauling away rubble and demolishing slums and kiosks, revving automobiles, trains and aeroplanes. Residents lived in disgusting unsanitary conditions. Noisome uncollected garbage abounded. Effluents from industries in the neighbourhood filled water bodies.

There was stagnant water and urine in gutters and drains serving as breeding grounds for mosquitos and flies virtually everywhere.

The atmosphere was foggy. This was the result of smoke and gaseous materials spewed out by trains, factories and trucks. Sometimes these noxious gases were disastrous. They resulted in the loss of thousands of human and animal life. They also contributed to the formation of acid rain which desolated plants' life.

The buildings were formidable tall skyscrapers, cathedrals, edifices and hovels constructed from newspapers, cartoons and parking crates. Occasionally, one spotted a flickering neon light. Then one read: Motel de Cavoite, L'hotel de Lust, Club D'eteste, L'hotel d Abomination, Death House, Carnal Buildings, Demonic Institute of Technical Research in Human Weaknesses. We also beheld a metamopsycholic plant, where a soul could be fitted with a new body.

For effective management of these diverse souls, the supreme Government of Gehenna used a very prudent method. Every new soul incarnated in Gehenna was registered and issued with an identification number. This was neither transferable nor exchangeable. All souls were known by their admission numbers. Finger prints, voice prints, denture, hair, birth marks were recorded. The souls were then freed. They would then settle down in their own styles. A file was immediately opened on each new soul. Spies were set on it. They collected data on it. Its amoral indulgences, degrees of incredibility, intelligence quotient, likes and dislikes and any other useful information. The data was then fed into a computer. This information could be used for tracing it, for blackmail or to get it to comply with certain governmental and anti-social conventions.

City dwellers lived much the same way as the inhabitants of Ahera. Drinking, drug pushing, feuding, flirting, revelling and wallowing in happy-go-lucky pursuits.

Other idlers were engaged in nuisance demonstrations, bearing placards with bold anti-establishment slogans.

In any direction one turned, one saw spaces of vandalism, sparked off by political, religious, racial and ethnocentric deviation. Bullet riddled bodies and mutilated decaying corpses lay all over the place, in the alleys and streets.

I wondered how one would cope with such an unfortunate, perfidious society. A penitent realisation dawned on me. I imagined myself proscribed in this den of infamy.

There were many recreation centres. Social amenities here were in an apologetic state. People amused themselves by watching soccer, rugby, judo and karate tournaments which they preferred to hard work. These activities always ended up with fans going wild. Deaths resulted.

Eventually the *Life* landed on the roof of Desideratum Building.

CHAPTER TEN

Wearing bizarre masks, we fought our way through dense human traffic. Occasionally, a pickpocket jostled against you. A watch got snatched, a wallet picked. Someone would be murdered or raped in the streets while the crowd just watched in apathy, or went about their own businesses nonchalantly.

We witnessed long queues of people waiting desperately to purchase essential commodities, which were ever in short supply. Hoarders and smugglers had a field day.

Among the crowds I recognized people I had known in the Herebefore but had long departed from the Earth. One of them was Libertine Mrembo; a distant cousin of mine. She had died after an abortion performed by an unauthorized, inexperienced private back street doctor. The pregnancy had not been her husband's. She had slept with her Asian boss. Everyone would know that she was unchaste. The Asian took her to the back street doctor. The other one was Shaft, alias Ransome Rukungu, a former schoolmate. He had swiftly climbed the ladder in the firm where he worked, purpotedly through nepotism. He was corrupt and took bribes. He loved alcohol and sex. When he suddenly died in mysterious circumstances, his multitude of widows and concubines surfaced to demand their share of inheritance. The ensuing wrangles delayed the burial. When he was finally buried in a marble-tilted grave he had dug earlier, his corpse had decomposed beyond recognition.

Others were people I had known only vaguely, or whose faces I had seen in the newspapers. People killed in road accidents or murdered. People shot down in gun-fire exchange with the police in robberies, some of them having rained terror in their home areas with their nihilistic activities. I tried to recall the details and circumstances surrounding their deaths. Two leading factors were accidents and disease.

Along the shop-fronts, beggars, in their uniforms of misery, displayed their deformity to maximum advantage. Some sang or wailed to attract the attention of passers-by. Homosexuals, prostitutes and travestites stood at street corners, soliciting for clients. Lunatics in rags, others utterly naked, moved up and down the streets, assaulting people and performing all sorts of antics. Children with wads of bank notes badgered people in a bid to exchange the currency. Any foreign exchange was acceptable.

71

There were many tunnels, underground streets, avenues and boulevards. These provided expedient venues for clandestine meetings for those working in the underworld: smugglers, saboteurs, assassins and thieves.

Here one saw shops dealing in human spare parts. Those who were in dire need for money could sell their organs. Blood was packed in special packs, classified and resold. Kidneys, livers, hearts and limbs were priced. Those daunting enough sold their conscience to feed their families. Scientists bought skeletons and other organs for their research. Consequently, many people, especially children disappeared mysteriously.

Cases were cited where patients were known to sell drugs prescribed by doctors. With the proceeds they bought cheaper palliatives or simply got drunk.

Eventually we came to 'Hotel Laissez-faire'. The atmosphere inside was stale with beer fumes, vomit, tobacco smoke, perspiration, perfume and toilet stench. The star-studded walls flashed all colours of the rainbow. The walls were decorated with grotesque paintings and porno signs.

The music was interspersed with magic shows, political speeches, concerts and film strips. The nude vocalist, high with drugs, displayed her gawdy jewellery and wriggled her body in the most provocative manner. The music was highly infectious. Her husky voice blared inordinately through the amplifiers. The song was *In The Middle of Nowhere*:

> *In the middle of nowhere,*
> *You, being your best companion,*
> *Away on a deserved holiday*
> *From all those cases, fears, misery,*
> *Agog for reconciliation*
> *With your best friend, yourself.*

> *In the middle of nowhere*
> *courting Ignorance and Bliss*
> *Free from all arduous planning*
> *The past so remote ....*
> *The present so fantastic ....*
> *The future so ecstatic.*

I'm happy to be here,
A world all my own,
No more hustle and bustle
Relaxation Galore ....
Rehabilitation Centre ....
In the middle of nowhere.

The boisterous revellers swayed in tune with the music like mari-onettes. They stamped their feet, whistled and cheered the nude vocalist.

The place seethed with spies, journalists and detectives. Marshal Gikuu warned us to be discreet.

The shelves behind the counter were crammed with merchandise. These comprised drinks, with peculiar names: Perdition, Penance, Sedition, Rock, Contraceptive Beer, Alcohol Inhaler and Sodhol. I sampled a bottle of Perdition. It knocked my brains instantly.

Other items included contraceptive chewing gum, aphrodisiacs in brands like: Afrodiscs, Libido, Power, Erotika and Sexomiac.

A girl, looking like a cosmetic advertisement, sauntered over to me.

"Hi, Handsome," she cooed, "I'm game."

I shook my head.

"For enjoyment," she persisted.

I declined.

"In the name of lust ..."

I ignored her. She walked off. On the back of her leather jacket was the inscription: *Sex Power!*

Honourable Nyoka, the incumbent MP for Ahera and the Minister for Social Services came on to the stage. He was the guest of honour. His rival, Taabu Leo, had been summarily detained. He had later died in prison.

"Ladies and gentlemen," he bellowed in the microphone, "I thank the organisers of this programme for conferring on me the award of Man of the Season. I also thank you for the award of 'the man with the highest record of marriages and divorces!' I believe I owe this to my good looks, wealth and charm, which most women find irresistible. But they bore me fast."

The audience clapped and cheered.

"Ladies and gentlemen," he continued, "above all, I'm very, very pleased to have this opportunity to give out the various awards of merit in various fields of human endeavours."

73

He turned to his prospectus.

"The State of Ghasia takes the first prize for leading in copulation and population and explosion!" Cheers. Drums. Whistling.

"The same state has the vastest arid land."

Confused murmurs.

"The people of Ghasia are at present experiencing certain difficulties which go hand in hand with over-population: education opportunities for school-age children, health facilities, water, good housing, employment for both skilled and unskilled manpower. The citizens of this over-populated state are presently experiencing a severe energy crunch. Essential commodities have varnished from shop counters. You can only get them on the black market at prohibitive prices."

There was mixed reaction in the audience.

"I'm particularly very proud to announce that we, the people of Ahera and the people of Ghasia are like brothers and sisters. We have been supplying them with aid: food, drugs, and skilled manpower. We have in fact, sent them expatriates, in a bid to help them to rehabilitate their economy."

Cheers. Drums and bugles. Whistling.

"The second award goes to the state of Dunia. This is the state where catachysmic fighting has been going on for ages. Through the initial fighting sparked off from political power, it has developed other reasons, conflicts control of mineral resources and aggression continue to sustain it. Ayatollah Mambo and the army commander, Pesa, will bear me witness."

More cheers.

At the signal from Marshal Gikuu, we drifted among the revellers past the noisy gambling machines and sex dens. We identified ourselves to a Mr. Lah-di-da at the reception desk. He ushered us through a heavily guarded corridor to Labyrinth Hall. The other members of the Creation nodded their greetings as we took our seats.

The conference opened with prayers, conducted by His Holiness the Pope Driftsham I.

"Dear friends," Professor Wiseman began after the prayer. "The object of this meeting is to review and appraise our progress vis-a-vis Operation Satan."

The members nodded and murmured in agreement.

"But let us first observe a minute's silence in the honour of the three members of the Creation who died in different accidents, while working on our various projects."

Silence.

"It's also poignantly touching that two of our top engineers went insane before completing an invention they had deviced," Wiseman continued after the silence, "Five others mysteriously went missing. We suspect that they were either spies or they simply defected when they realized the enormity of the task at hand."

The professor went on to pay glowing tribute to all the members of the Creation for their commitment and devotion. For their willingness to jeopardise their lives in their endeavour to improve the lot of mankind.

Pope Driftsham I spoke with aplomb. He recounted how he had worked ceaselessly and urged the church to work tirelessly towards total emancipation of mankind. He had urged the various groups whom he had addressed to contribute generously. To support the Creation materially, spiritually and morally. He observed that no human being could claim to be perfect. It was through divine retribution that we were in Gehenna. Only through divine absolution could we be freed.

Another speaker, a leading researcher, Mr. Brovsky, elucidated how the industrial accidents, mentioned by Wiseman had occurred, and how three engineers had perished and numerous other workers maimed.

He then produced satellite photographs of the bases from which nuclear missiles against Satan would be launched. When he finished he laid his report before Dr. Felicitus Web, Creation's Secretary-General.

Marshal Gikuu made a report on his reconnaissance at the Mausoleum, the previous night. He outlined the details of the layout of it and the environs. He confirmed Professor Wiseman's previous report on the installations. He, too, produced photographs and sketches to illustrate his observations.

Senior Private Keega presented our joint report. This was on polarisation of the power that operated on the robots and 'vigilante' equipment. We had compiled this report in collaboration with Trixy Waruo and Lubaina.

Dr. Felicitus Web, still in her perennial beauty, made a report on the information gleaned from collaboration in various quarters.

Professor Femines Tabasamu, the women's leader, spoke of women's participation in Creation. The bulk of women, who formed more than half of the population in Gehenna, pledged, to work side by side with their male counterparts. They sincerely hoped that after the struggle was won, they would share equal rights with men. They hoped to see an end to sex discrimination in politics, the economy and social affairs. They had held conferences in various places to renew their collective spirit.

Juvenile Kijana, short-sighted, partially deaf and physically robust, was the youth leader. He announced that the majority of youngsters supported the Creation whole-heatedly. He had heeded the elder's advice to instil a sense of morale, discipline and confidence in the youth. He thanked the entire Creation for guiding the youth to acquire intellectual, social, spiritual, moral and physical skills to enable them to become self-reliant and contribute positively to the development and maintenance of society.

Many other members spoke. Some had nothing useful to say. They spoke because they liked to hear their own voices. They were courteously thanked and asked to sit down. Others congratulated Wiseman on his discovery of herbs and roots which could be used, instead of rats and rabbits, to establish viability of certain drugs in treating human diseases.

Others thanked Mr. Brovsky for inventing equipment that would enable the souls of the dead to communicate with the living on Earth.

It was also disclosed that Professor Wiseman and Mr. Brovsky, with their students were at an advanced stage of establishing a drug which would render kidney operations unnecessary. They had already published successful discoveries on the cure for AIDS, chronic syphilis and other milder cases of Sexually Transmitted Diseases.

"Comrades," the professor spoke from his wonderful wheelchair, "You have done a commendable job. With this gallant spirit, we shall achieve our goal and liberate both Gehenna and Earth; indeed the entire universe from the shackles of the Devil."

"Sir," Mr. Brovsky interposed, "In our assessment, everything seems ready. There are a lot of protests against our nuclear pollution, radio-active wastes and cramming the space with junk in the course of preparing for the onslaught. The environment is in danger! When do we launch the attack?"

"Fine," replied the professor. "In that case we should not delay. Is it okay if we set our zero hour for October 23, 2052?"

The suggestion was unanimously adopted.

The eclipse cast a glum over the city. Electric lights flickered on. People danced in the streets. At the crowded city market, an irate jilted constable lost his head. He opened machine gun fire on the throng, killing several people and wounding others critically.

A ghastly accident occurred on Carnage Avenue. All passengers, who had been packed like sardines, died instantly. Good Samaritans wielded axes and hammers in a bid to free the mangled bodies in the wrecked metal contraption. Some sympathisers happily salvaged the blood-stained luggage. They ransacked the corpses for any valuable jewellery, shoes and money.

A bomb ripped through the Cannibian Embassy. Terrorists fled from the blazing building, bundling frightened hostages into a waiting helicopter. They escaped. In their wake, they left a volley of bullets, corpses, casualties and a dazed crowd. A television crew had been set up in advance for a live recording of the incident.

My mind was precariously boggled by the traumatic panorama of events.

Pandemonium broke when it started raining acid. People scurried for cover. Buildings started crashing down.

"Fire! He-l-p!" the confused crowd hollered.

The inferno increased.

Through a strange stroke of luck, we managed to reach Desideratum Building. Marshal Gikuu steered *Life* over Shamblesville and through the corrosive rain.

Down below us, buildings crumbled and crushed stampeding pedestrians and motorists. There were anguished cries, as people struggled to flee from the scene.

We witnessed all this suffering with a mingled sense of sorrow and consternation. Gikuu informed us that these occurrences had long ceased to worry the inhabitants of Gehenna. To them they had become the order of the day.

At long last, the *Life* came down and spread out its springy legs. Before getting off the craft, Gikuu gave us all the pictures we had taken.

We watched the enormous metallic insect and waved at it until if faded into the distance.

"Boy!" Keega sighed as we walked towards the Mausoleum. "It was a helluva day."

"That, it was!" I conceded.

CHAPTER ELEVEN

We were caught in a raging thunderstorm. Lightning flashed. Eerie objects appeared in the sky. A gust of wind uprooted huge trees, blocking our way.

We stumbled and clambered over the barriers. Thorns slashed us. The entire environment reverberated with strange and forbidding noises from frightened animals. Unidentifiable forms dispersed in all directions. We were overwhelmed with fear ... fear of the unknown.

"Gosh!" Keega muttered, "What's all this now?"

"I, too, am in the dark," I answered with chattering teeth. "It's even worse than the first day, isn't it?"

"Let us hasten to get to the Mausoleum."

At that juncture, our radio crackled on. The reception was poor. We had to strain our ears to hear.

"Do you read me, over."

"Beacon responding to Terminator. We read you faintly. Caught in a storm, over."

"Terminator to Beacon and Best. Calling in *Life* from space, over. Bad news. Devil raging. Wisdom dead. Aircrash over Liberty mountains. *Aluta continua*."

"We copy you, sir, " I replied in a tearful voice.

"Terminator to Beacon and Best. Over and out."

Keega nodded his head sadly to show he got the ominous news of the death of Professor Wiseman.

In pain, confusion and remorse, we sloshed through the puddles, water from our hairs stinging our eyes. We experienced difficulty in breathing.

Chaos greeted us in the Mausoleum. Lights were dimmed. The place seemed deserted. The furniture was broken and stripped. Articles were scattered all over the place. Tattered women's clothes were carelessly thrown about.

We surveyed the sordid parlour with bated breath, shivering with cold and wet, our minds totally befuddled.

Suddenly, a blood-curdling scream shattered the eerie silence, sending chills down my spine. The building shook, as if rocked by a mighty tremor. The windows and doors rattled. More items tumbled from the shelves to the floor. Without volition, as if impelled by a force more than our own will-power, we found ourselves groping in the dark along the whispering walls.

The hubbub grew louder as we approached Confessional. We heard ecstatic voices, like those of people speaking in tongues. The strident cries of babies and children.

We halted at the open door, spellbound.

The randy congregation pranced about and limped round in circles inside a crude design of a square circle. They were utterly naked. They brandished short sharp spears, knives, clubs, rubber whips, and metal bars. They were frantically engrossed in a ritual dance. They cut themselves. Blood gushed from their veins. They screamed. Hollered. Hurt each other. They intoned prayers and abracadabra to the Prince of Darkness. They pledged their souls. Cursed God!

The hall was filled with a thick cloud of black smoke. The hysterical worshippers seemed to be completely oblivious to the obnoxious odours exuding from a vast cauldron on a huge fire in the room. Black candles burnt intermittently, giving begrudged light and casting weird shadows on the walls.

Satan sat with his senior aides in the altar. His Hot-Seat burnt sprightly in the splendid flames behind him, on the wall hung a sign written in tongues of fire:

> *HIS EXISTENCE ALMIGHTY SATAN LUCIFER,*
> *LORD OF THE UNIVERSE — HELL AND EARTH*
> *MASTER OF ALL THAT EXISTS*
> *VISIBLE AND INVISIBLE*
> *THAT WAS, IS AND WILL BE.*

Above it was a broken cross hanging loosely upside-down.

The high priest and priestess spoke in strange tongues. Their bodies trembled in prayers. Mothers held up their babies to be cursed. Cripples threw away their crutches in fury. The blind defied darkness and crushed into people or the macabre objects in the hall. Everybody bawled out blasphemies and obscenities.

The priests and priestesses screamed and curved signs of their faithfuls' stomachs, shaving the women completely bald.

As the frenzy built up, they babbled incoherent incantations. They sprinkled the unholy gathering with the blood of white horses, black cats,

79

venomous snakes and human beings. Bats, owls, serpents and vampires mingled freely with the worshippers. Huge poisonous spiders crawled along their labyrinthine webs among the bizarre crowd.

After offering human sacrifices, the ritual culminated in sexual orgies and gore. The place was worse than a madhouse. Watching it all was a harrowing experience.

At the command of Bel-el-zebul, the commotion subsided and the crowd slumped down on the linoleum floor, exhausted; some foaming from the mouth. Satan Lucifer became more conspicuous. He loomed mighty, smug, powerful and enigmatic. Occasionally, he laughed, or relayed orders to his cohorts near the alter. Just by a sheer look and the message would be perceived, through telepathy.

Presently, the interminable table before him was laid. Infinite epicurean dishes were served. Satan invited his party. They gorged themselves with great relish. Music filled the air. Dancers suddenly emerged. Fire flames whipped among them. The dance was called "The Snake."

The protean atmosphere abruptly took a traumatic turn.

Heads of the various states of Gehenna rose. They diffidently approached the throne, prostrated themselves before Lucifer and lauded him for his power, wealth, achievements and Satanic wisdom. In similar blandishment they continued to read their memoranda. They brought him presents of money, gold and souls. Most of them adopted a similar formula:

> *"Hail, Satan!"*
> *"Hail the Devil!"*
> *"Satan Lives!"*
> *"Death Survives!"*
> *"The Realm of Darkness!"*
> *"Kingdom Everlasting!"*
> *"Victory for us, Evil triumphs."*

They would then proceed to read reports on their political murders, extortion of their subjects, detention without trial, food dumping in seas or burning in order to keep prices high. Price increases on essential goods. Diversion of natural resources into personal private property. Wanton expenditure from the state coffers creating economic hardships which resulted in chronic crimes and lawlessness. Robberies, murders, rape and the ilk.

80

Others narrated their expertise in electoral fraudulence, political tricks and dictatorship. They recounted ruthless methods of dealing with dissidents.

Some were praised. Others were condemned. Before long, the floor was littered with corpses. Some were impaled on hot iron stakes, others gunned down or cursed to death.

Satan laconically meted out the sentence after hearing the charges. None was granted that privilege of defending himself. It was sentence without trial.

"Electrocute him. Gas chamber. Crucify him. Hang him. Scaffold injection. Remand him in scorpion infested underground dungeon. Acidify him. Torturing wheels. Hammer him. Poison Sharks. Burning tyres ..."

Everyone screamed and struggled vociferously with the guards when they heard their fate. The armed guards on their part, were fast in execution of their duties.

As the number of the congregation dwindled relentlessly, we could make out the accused shadows, paintings and writings on the wall. Our eyes had gradually got accustomed to the bleary lighting in the Confessional. We could recognise some of the faces which were so unceremoniously marshalled before the throne of the 'Vain-glory'. We had slightly recovered from our initial shock.

The two ladies who were dragged before Satan wore masks of horror and terror. Their obdurate prosecutors followed in their wake. A tall, husky, stubbly bearded figure with misshappen features. He stepped forward brusquely to deliver his testimony.

"Challenge!" Keega and I uttered in unison. We huddled together, shivering trying to control our chattering teeth.

We listened.

Trixy Waruo, Lubaina Zawadi Igbo and others not before the 'Judgement Seat' were accused of high treason. They had acted in a manner detrimental to the good kingdom of Gehenna by leaking highly classified and confidential information to members of a clandestine force whose heinous motives were to wreck the Kingdom of Satan. They were also charged with plotting to assassinate Satan Lucifer, the Sovereign and the sole legitimate ruler of Gehenna and its vassals. The said persons were also accused of sabotage, insurbordination, subversion and supporting dangerous and erroneous religious doctrines.

81

He disclosed that Secret and Thought Police had extorted confessions from the suspects. They had used all available means including exotic drugs, which aided co-operation. There were also the defectors. They had broken their moratorium for silence.

Among Challenge's exhibits were the dead bodies of the engineers who had died in the accidents. The mangled, grotesque remains of Professor Wiseman. Challenge's malignant face surveyed the incensed throng, then the nebulous authority at the altar. We almost screamed when he turned round superciliously and glared at us with his evil, beastly eyes. He leered portentously.

"My Lord, Satan Lucifer," he rasped in the voice of doom. "Let it be known by all rational beings. The Kingdom of Gehenna under your able and wise leadership is absolutely invincible. It cannot be intimidated by any mortal efforts."

The fiendish crowd cheered tumultuously.

The verdict was lucidly meted out. Lubaina Zawadi was condemned to immediate old age. Challenge stirred some concoction with a human limb and served her in a human skull. She was forced to drink. She gurgled it down her throat. Her eyes closed. Instantaneously, her face became grooved with wrinkles. She bent forward, her legs too weak to support her. She slumped. Sat down on the floor, utterly helpless with age. Her previously beautiful hair turned into an ugly white wig. She shrunk. I heard Keega groaning painfully.

Trixy Waruo would be sacrificed. This, apparently, would absolve Satan and his allies from all the atrocities they had committed that night. Satan would eat her heart. The others her brain, liver, kidneys and drink her blood. Challenge pulled out a knife from its scabbard. Spontaneously, his earlier murder by Gikuu flashed through my mind.

She screamed. In my voice.

Her entrails; intestines, kidneys, liver and blood gushed out. Everything began revolving before me at a terrific speed. My whole body was ground by a strange machine before I collapsed.

CHAPTER TWELVE

What a curse a bed could be, even when made of pure gold and fancy bedding; yet one cannot fall asleep in it!

Throughout the night, I tossed and turned, writhing a rhythm of pain in my whole being.

At times there were stealthy scratching noises against the walls. These would be closely followed by undecipherable echoes. Then morbid howls which would ultimately become deafening.

There were other times when the air felt heavy. It became difficult to breathe. I panted, gasped and sucked in the suffocating air.

When, eventually, sleep drowned me, it was only to dream of macabre mysteries; blood curdling orgies and treachery. The eternal night dragged on.

I woke up at dawn to find myself curled up in bed like a malformed foetus in the womb. The feather pillow had slid to the floor. My head lay in a mess of bloody vomit. I was still in my drenched clothes. There was a putrid taste in my mouth. The agony became intolerable. My spirit reached a nadir. I contemplated suicide. The 'Death Cords' in the bedroom wall came to mind. I needed only to choose between gas poisoning and suffocation.

I struggled to sit up. Abruptly I felt the bed whirling like a merry-go-round. I felt sick. When the dizziness abated, I surveyed the two lethal cords with my watch light. The temptation of death became overwhelmingly tantalizing and pleasurable. I radioed Keega to solicit his support and to bid him farewell. I felt almost ashamed to opt for this cowardly course and abandon my best friend to his own fate.

"Keega, Kimuri speaking," I groaned.

"Hello, Kimuri," Keega replied faintly, "How are you, brother?"

"Terrible, brother. The pain. Can't stand it."

"Yes?" he enquired with alarm.

"The 'Death Cords,' I'll kill myself."

"What?"

"It's hell, brother. Unbearable," I persisted.

"Don't talk like that," Keega reproached in a voice charged with emotion. "Bosh. I, too, am suffering, man."

He paused. Waited. I said nothing.

"We shouldn't think so diffidently," he spoke laboriously.

"I'm sorry."

"Kimuri, don't. Okay?"

"Yes …"

"You shouldn't forget we're invaluable assets to the Creation. We have pledged ourselves for the arduous task. As long as we are alive we shall go on with it. I will die with you."

"I, too, will die with you."

"Brother, let's stick together. Over and out."

"Yes …" I whispered feebly.

The pain was resuming with renewed potency.

I was startled out of sleep by the violent crash of the door. Gloria Gallows stormed into the room, her face livid with fury and hate. She was stark naked. Her long copper red hair let down carelessly, gave her curvacious body a weird appearance. Her eyes burnt with an evil glint. Her tattooed body was scarred and coated with congealed blood from the satanic rituals of the previous night. Apparently she was still dazed with drugs.

"Filth!" she yelled at me. "You should be ashamed of yourself. Rolling in corruption like a swine!"

I made an attempt to protest. No voice. I couldn't talk!

I clenched my teeth against the pain. Tears of mortification rolled down my cheeks. It astounded me how people liked condemning others for the very evils they themselves perpetrated. Those who were weak were always made the scapegoats.

Gloria continued to denigrate me relentlessly.

"Our loyalty to our master is unwavering. Unquestionable! But you …"

She spate derisively.

"You've been behaving so arrogantly because of those bitches. That's why you've scorned us. You've been denying us gratification and entered into conspiracy with them. Enough of that. Traitors."

She spat again, venom.

As the tarmagant went on raving and boasting about her unflinching loyalty to devils, my nerves became frazzled. My vision blurred. Gloria looked monstrous. Frightening!

Suddenly, I became a blind-and-deaf mute.

When I came to, I found myself stretched beside Keega on a frayed coach in the squalid parlour. Satan Lucifer, the 'Dread Monarch', was lolling regally in his great throne — The Hot Seat. In spite of his nocturnal exertions, he still looked cheerful and relaxed.

"Good morning, sons of men," he smiled at us dubiously. "Come on, now. Rally your will to live."

Finding it perplexing to meet his searching gaze, I rolled my eyes tardily round the room. It was still dirty and disorganized.

"Never mind the house, Kimuri," Satan admonished. "The maids have gone on strike. Two of them have absconded."

Waruo and Zawadi came to my mind. I suspected the lie was told to bluff us from enquiring about their sudden disappearance.

"The robots, too, have been temporarily de-activated."

This last disclosure jerked us into alertness. What was Satan driving at? Gloria Gallows, in her outburst had indicated there was evidenced that we, like Waruo and Zawadi, were members of the clandestine movement known as the Creation. And it was for this reason the two ladies had been liquidated. How safe were we?

"But why, sir?" Keega enquired hoarsely. "I mean why have they absconded?"

"A change of life," Satan offered. "Now, to put you back into your real selves take this …"

He popped open two phials. Keega and I exchanged furtive glances. Our suspicion intensified.

"No, thank you, sir," I said.

"Not again …," Keega came in.

"Come on, you need it badly," Satan rejoined.

That took me back to the incident at the River of Death. At any rate we wouldn't like to antagonize our host too soon. The zero hour 2052 was still far off.

"Alright," I assented, boldly taking the phial. Keega also took his reluctantly. We drained the contents. Almost instantaneously, we felt immensely refreshed. Revitalized. Everything in the parlour, which had previously looked gloomy and bleak took a new image. Everything appeared exotic. The broken furniture. The battered crockery. The rags. The wilting flowers that had wafted deathly odours. The sagging skulls on the walls, crocked with age. Our eccentric, unconventional and debonair

85

host whose ambient personality seemed to permeate every aspect of the surrounding. Everything! They all suddenly took on attractive appearance.

We started to warm up towards our saviour, Satan.

I leapt into the air and impulsively embraced Keega.

"Thank you, sir," Keega said gratefully.

"Oh, that's alright," Satan reposed, "I enjoy solving challenging problems."

"What went wrong with us?" I enquired.

"Imbalance of bodily functions. Something very dangerous. It could be fatal. You allow yourselves to suffer too much physical and emotional stress."

"But, Sir," I reasoned. "It is difficult to watch all the suffering we have observed here without being adversely affected."

"Sir," Keega joined in, "I wonder who could be responsible for all this suffering?"

"Man," Satan asserted.

"How?" I prodded.

"Man is a most powerful, intelligent, devious and destructive force. He revels in heaping contumely on his fellow men. All this he does in the name of public interest, security, development and freedom."

"But sir, man on his part blames Satan for the mess in which he finds himself." Keega argued.

"Precisely. Man will always find a scapegoat for his vice. He will always want to justify himself," Satan responded. "Now let's watch the news."

He punched a button on the table. Darkness fell. The signature tune played. The news followed.

From the wall in front of us came an explosion followed by billowing clouds of smoke, then an inferno. Amidst the zealous crackling from the blazing buildings were horrified screams.

The newscaster announced that property of an unknown value, and invaluable records were destroyed. It was suspected that the arsonists could have been some senior government officers or bank directors in a bid to cover up their acts of mismanagement and embezzlement. Charred corpses of workers trapped in the building had been recovered in the debris; most of them burnt beyond recognition.

"In Ghasia, armed police assisted by paramilitary forces battled for the seventh day with irate masses protesting over the new food prices. Many government offices and residential homes have been destroyed. There has also been widespread looting.

"This came in the wake of the new budgetary proposals read to the parliament by the Minister for Finance and Economic Development, Professor Kikulacho. The Minister informed a hushed house that these austere measures are inevitable. The country has to meet its budgetary deficits, service its debts and cope with soaring inflation.

"The Minister admitted that some of the measures he has adopted are at the instigation of the Interstate Monetary Fund (IMF). The IMF is seen by many politicians and economists as an imperialist investment of the developed states to manipulate, exploit and control the economies of developing states," he paused.

On the screen could be seen the pathetic crowd on stampede. Brutal policemen in combat gear, wielding batons and shooting tear-gas canisters were in hot pursuit. A huge number of the sick, the aged, pregnant women and young children were trampled to death.

"Air travel has become increasingly insecure in the recent times," the announcer continued. "Three passenger planes caught fire and exploded in mid-air yesterday afternoon. In each incidents high explosive had gone off. Six hundred and seventy three passengers were killed in all. In separate incidents two other planes were hijacked. All the passengers were exterminated when their governments refused to accede to the hijackers' demands. These included exchanging the hostages with certain criminal elements serving long terms in jail. They also expected huge sums of money and weapons.

"The Government of Dunia has called on the Cannibian Government to submit for re-trial the captain of *Doomsday* and his crew for hurling twenty six passengers overboard into the shark infested Corruption Seas. The culprits stood trial in a Cannibian court two years ago and were acquitted for lack of evidence. They were, however later jailed for six months each to appease the universal hue and cry. The Dunia authorities saw this as a travesty of justice.

"Over three million people have died this year from traffic and industrial accidents alone. This was disclosed by Police Traffic Headquarters in Shamblesville. Drivers have been advised to refrain from driving under the influence of drugs. Bhang, heroine, cocaine and alcohol were

87

cited among others. Discourtesy, illness, drowsiness and age were also said to contribute to accidents.

"An unknown number of people lost their lives in a motley of catastrophes that struck Gehenna yesterday in the afternoon. These ranged from earthquakes that felled huge buildings, crashing pedestrians and motorists, to volcanic eruptions that emitted obnoxious gases and floods. Hospitals reported cases of strange, hitherto unknown diseases that they could not treat.

"Christians all over the Kingdom of Gehenna celebrated their Christmas this October. This is an important occasion commemorating the nativity of Jesus Christ — who was crucified by men for his revolutionary view of the world and his endeavour to save mankind from what his followers call 'the shackles of sin and the power of evil.'

"To the majority of people, both Christians and non-Christians, Christmas is a time for extravagance, immorality and destruction. Many families go out on spending sprees. Many homes are broken into. A copious number of human lives are lost through family feuds, drunken brawls, and terrorism. Many domestic animals lose their lives too. Their carcasses are relished to highlight the occasion. A majority of destitute families, nonetheless, never known the difference between Christmas, Idd Ul Fitr, Diwali or National days. They just watch the whole thing with awe and gratefully accept whatever generosity might be thrown to them.

"With the approaching new year, many states are still saddled with the problems of inflation. Many states have also reported massive unemployment, famine, debt quagmire, economic shambles, political strife and friction between the Church and the State."

These wrangles have immensely contributed to moral decadence, spiritual lethargy and spates of violent crime and blackmarkets flourishing with all kinds of wares that can no longer be bought over the shop counter.

"A number of governments have been called upon to resign before being forcibly toppled. At the same time, over the past few months, there have been a number of assassination attempts on various heads of states. They presume to know what is best for their subjects, while hiding behind the facade of democracy. Once in power they never want to share or relinquish it.

"It has come to light that there are certain clandestine movements with motives to overthrow Satan's regime. Leaders from all states of Gehenna

88

issued strong statements condemning disgruntled elements behind these movements, as well as their foreign masters. Their activities are being closely monitored. They have been advised to come forward and give themselves up to the authorities before they are named in public."

The news — the Gospel of Gehenna — was closely followed by an outburst of music and slogans, adulating Satan Lucifer and the Kingdom of Gehenna.

CHAPTER THIRTEEN

That horrid news reel left us fervently perturbed. We were overwhelmed with commiseration. Keega and I found ourselves impulsively moaning and muttering protests.

"Cruel!"

"Sadistic,"

"Tyrannical,"

"Savagery,"

"Utterly malevolent!"

After the broadcast, Satan Lucifer switched off the darkness. We eyed each other in portentous silence. Keega, like me, was having difficulty in dissembling his anguish.

"Now, gentlemen," Satan probed cheerily, "What do you say about it?"

"Ignominious," Keega replied, indignantly.

"And where did you see Satan in all that?"

We paused. Pondered thoughtfully. We had to be circumspect. We could not say anything disagreeable for fear of reprisals. I wondered if we had made any inadvertent disclosures in our delirious ejaculations. If Satan could dispense with members of his retinue so ruthlessly as he had done earlier in our very presence, was it not much easier for him to liquidate us, and nobody would get wise to what happened to us?

My mind once again harked back to the time we had arrived to Gehenna. All that we had witnessed. Experienced. Learnt. From Satan himself. From Trixy Waruo and Zawadi. From Marshal Gikuu and members of the Creation. Satan's premise was that all human suffering, usually attributed to him, was, by far and large a direct consequence of man's own deeds and misdeeds or those of his fellow man.

I recalled the petty jealousies. The wrangles and the fights we had had in the Mausoleum. The debauchery and the dissipation with the maids. The activities in the Confessional the previous night. Vendetta, mutilations, profanities, cannibalism and necrophilia. The abject poverty and squalor which had reduced the inhabitants of Ahera to a state of grovelling beasts, while their illiberal leaders and their cronies were frantically busy. Busy amassing wealth. Wealth to ensure they remained in power indefinitely. Power through intrigue and intimidation. And force!

90

The new super-technology, we had observed, was used to procure negative ends; devastating and pernicious to the welfare of mankind. These included creation of monstrosities in the laboratory. Hermaphrodites, with both male and female genders. Sexless creatures. Sex change operations were surgically performed to transform males into females and vice versa. These experimentations went further to produce creatures with multiplex heads and grotesque appearances. Belligerent beings, ready to tear each other asunder on sight.

New diseases were contrived to defeat all known cures. Highly contagious diseases that maimed gradually but effectively. Diseases that were inexorably transmitted to the posterity.

Dangerous chemicals were sold to farmers with the malicious motive of poisoning their crop and retarding their yields. These chemicals polluted both the air and the soil. The contaminated products were injurious to the consumers' health.

Mendacious advertisements were transmitted through the mass media, encouraging the gullible public to indulge in drug abuse, smoking and compulsive alcoholism. This created fractatious demand for substandard commodities, promoted pornography and propaganda.

The super-power game of arms-race confused the priorities of the sycophant states. Instead of giving them badly needed development aid to enable them to be self-reliant in food production and economically innovative, they sold them weapons. Ultra-modern missiles. They instigated wars which devastated whole nations and continents.

I thought of man-made famine; where food was hoarded or confiscated. Crops burnt. Whole families were subjected to starvation. Untold millions perished from hunger while food was exported abroad and state coffers defrauded.

Yes, Shamblesville, Newtown, Rottingden, Destruction City. The conurbation of cosmopolitan cities quintessence of the modern jungle. Here all Mahatma Gandhi's principles were shattered with ardent impunity. People ravished:

> *Politics without principles*
> *Wealth without work*
> *Pleasure without conscience*
> *Commerce without morality*

Worship without sacrifice
Science without humanity.

Well, well, well. Satan Lucifer: the Tempter. The Liar. The Slanderer. The Adversary. The Devil! To borrow only a few of his innumerable sobriquets. To incite every soul to err, at least at some time, of their existence. He must definitely be exceedingly cunning. Omniscient, Omnipotent, and even, Omnipresent.

Paradoxically, though, Satan was astoundingly popular, influential and, as we had already witnessed, versatile and indefatigably industrious!

"Gentlemen," Satan shattered the Ominous silence, "You seem to revel in gloomy predilections"

"But sir," I answered miserably, "We have conscience."

"Sure," Keega supported, "We empathize with the plight of the damned souls."

"Fine," Satan said stoically. "I quite clearly understand your compassion. But you needn't get so maudlin."

We kept silent.

"Right, then. What are you doing to improve their situation?"

"Nothing, sir," I mumbled in alarm.

"Really?" Satan said smugly. "Passivity, apathy, diffidence and lethargy lead to a very hopeless state of affairs."

"What should we do?" Keega enquired.

"Be strong. Courageous. Tolerant. Relaxed."

"Then?" I coaxed.

"Be realistic. Alter what you can. Endure what you can't," he hastily added.

"Sympathy alone is no solution to any problem. You're just poisoning your minds. Infecting yourselves with negative emotions."

"Sir," Keega said despondently, "Are you suggesting we should develop insouciance and callousness?"

"Nope. But before we endeavour to change things, it's imperative to ensure that people have an explicit idea about the sort of world you intend to build for them."

"Meaning?" I asked.

"Meaning that at times revolutionaries endeavour to liberate people who do not even know that they need any liberating," Satan Explained.

"But, sir," I enquired ruefully. "Why do you allow all this suffering?"

"Democracy." Satan parried.

"Uh?" Keega and I gasped.

"Liberty, men. Man has free will," Satan expostulated easily, "He knows and does what, to him, would help him to attain his ultimate good."

We looked at him, bewildered. He smiled smugly.

"Interestingly, however, man's ideas are usually inadequate and confused. So, man starts wars with a view to conquering and subjugating his fellow man. Man commits crime for the sake of adventure and self-aggrandizement. Man cheats in business, hankering for profits. Man indulges in mob justice as an orgiastic expiation of his guilt. Man destroys the environment, considering only his immediate needs."

I nodded grimly. At last I could see sense in what he was saying.

"Man indulges in obnoxious habits harmful to his health and that of his fellow man. He hurts himself and his neighbour. Is it in order to blame Satan for the consequences of what man does?"

We were confused. We said nothing.

"Consider the arms-race and its concomitant scandals. Its effects. The dumping of missiles in developing states. Misrule by depraved leaders."

We considered.

"Yes, sir," I couldn't help agreeing with him.

"Now, turn to religious institutions. They contribute to chaos and fanatic anarchism."

"How, sir?" we asked, astonished.

"The clergy dabble in politics. They are easily swayed by the rich. The powerful. They oppose and challenge the previously held church doctrines. They solemnize marriage annulments and support abortion and homosexuality. Many religious leaders are murderers and conspirators, philanderers and heretics. And you know what?"

"Mmh?"

"There are many people who have turned to religion to conceal their previous misdeeds. Others even use the religious facade to divert peoples' attention from their nefarious activities."

"True, sir," we assented.

Ecclesiastical institutions have been used to perpetuate racial supremacy, caste systems, war-mongering and superstition."

"And how, sir, would you explain the rancorous conflicts between the

93

religious institutions and the state?"

"Easy, my man. That's caused by conflict of interests. Both the religious institutions and the state are trying to have the upper hand over man's destiny."

While Satan continued thus in his sweet mellifluous voice and disarming smiles, I noticed yet another quality of his. That he was quite good at casuistry.

"Not that conflicts in themselves are bad. But man in his eagerness to assert he is right forgets that truth is multi-facetted, hence there are many approaches to the truth."

"Would you say then they fight for the truth?" Keega pursued.

"They might think so. Deluding themselves. Building their premises on prejudices, dead values and half-truths. Half-truth is no truth. Truth is able to look after itself."

I felt my head reeling. Getting more confused. The air in the parlour felt acrid.

"Then, of course, besides man's contribution to his suffering, there are natural causes. Even to these man does lend a helping hand by contaminating the ecosystem with industrial effluence and nuclear-fallout."

We nodded in awe.

"True," Satan said sabre-rattlingly, "I have the power to influence man's destiny. However, I prefer to leave him to his own devices."

CHAPTER FOURTEEN

The horrendous experiences in the Mausoleum only helped to aggravate our sense of foreboding.

The first was the fortuitous discovery of *The Pact*. A meticulously hand-written document concealed between the cover and the jacket of the book — The Satanic Bible.

"Grace! What the hell could this mean?" I asked Keega.

"Extremely baffling," he replied.

We scanned the astonishing document.

It was inscribed on gold paper. All along the four margins were designs of miniature skulls and skeletons of men, bats, scorpions, salamanders, spiders, owls and other ungodly creatures.

The text read:

> *"On my whole being; body, mind, soul, fortune and honour, I solemnly plead and swear that I will always be a committed disciple and servant of Satan, devoting my all, unsparingly, to sow seeds of discord and rebellion, evil and confusion in the universe and in the minds of the entire creation and shall never under any circumstances fail to abide by this oath of allegiance or, in any circumstances divulge any secrets that might jeopardize the Kingdom, or use the influence of the Kingdom for my personal interests, advertisements or aid of our stupendous rivals. If I do so, I realize, I do it at my own risk and peril in this life after life.*
>
> *I pledge to do all in my power to perpetuate the influence and powers of darkness. May all that is good, righteous and holy perish. May all that is evil and pernicious prevail.*
>
> *Hail Satan!*
> *Evil triumphs!*
> *As in the past, now and always;*
> *So be it.*

By the time we finished the third reading of *The Pact*, my pulse was hammering. My head ached with confusion.

95

What exactly did Satan want with us? What hideous powers, what diabolic perversity had led us on this ominous trajectory to Gehenna?

"Brother," Keega cautioned, "we'll have to be very careful."

"Now, why do you think *The Pact* had to be written in read?" I scrutinized it.

"Oh, it's not even ink. I think it's normally inscribed in the victim's blood.

We promptly signalled the document to Marshal Gikuu through our contact watches.

"Bravo, officers," he said happily, "You are doing a fine job."

"Do you suppose we, too, might be expected to sign a contract?"

"Possibly," he answered. "Our man is ruthlessly devious and capable of anything. Be careful.".

"Do you know of people who might have signed such a contract?" Keega enquired.

"Yes, several, in fact. Dr. Faustus, a German. Sold his soul to the Devil for material acquisition. Then there was Father Grandier, a French priest."

"Yeah, yeah. Satan told us about Dr. Faustus. Who was Father Grandier?"

"A French cure. A satyr. He readily fucked all the sex-starved nuns in his convent. The more he gave them the works, the more they wanted. Some even began seeking satisfaction in the streets. A Cardinal who was probably overwhelmed with jealousy owing to his avowed chastity found fault with Father Grandier. They charged him before a consistory with practising witchcraft in his seduction. Those invalid, aged, ugly and frigid nuns Father Grandier had scorned offered evidence against him. They even produced an affidavit purportedly signed between Father Grandier and the Devil. They tortured him to death."

"Who tortured him?" Keega pursued.

"His fellow clerics, of course."

"Just wanted to be sure."

"Fine."

"Are there any similar cases?" I probed. I wanted to know what we, too, could expect.

"Plenty. Some affecting clergy. Others laymen. And you know what?" Gikuu offered gratuitously.

"We're listening," I encouraged.

96

"These parties signed the contracts either for material excellence or sating their lusts for sex, power or violence. When they ultimately realized what such a treaty entailed, they may have wanted to renege or contravene it. In such circumstances of course, they would contrive tricks aimed at warding Satan off their tracks. In all cases he proved too wily for their machinations. The souls always ended in Gehenna, in accordance with the terms of the contracts."

"Thank you, sir, for the information," I said on behalf of Keega and myself.

"*Aluta continua*, Major Kimuri and Major Keega. Over and out."

Supernatural terrorism. It all started when Major Keega and I closed ourselves in bedlam — my bedroom to pray to God.

The atmosphere changed abruptly. There was a hurricane. The windows crashed and shattered. Objects in the room were viciously hurled at us by invisible forces. We sustained injuries. Blood spluttered. Screams in panic. hollering and fighting. The whole Mausoleum was inundated with black cats. Scrawny and mangy. All of them moaning. Caterwauling. Crawling and climbing against the wall glaring at us with evil luminous yellow eyes.

The air was suffused with an abominable stench of putrifaction.

"Demons!" Keega yelled in exasperation.

"What do we do?" I moaned.

"Death cords, brother," Keega suggested.

"Yeah, man."

I dived over the bedstead for the cords and tugged. All those lethal gases seeped into the room. The bedstead tossed me off. I stumbled, crashed into the drinks cabinet, sprang to my feet and smashed a charging feline.

"Scram!" Keega shrilled, yanking the door open. We bolted off to 'Pandemonium' — Keega's bedroom. Working frantically, we lit some charm powder that filled the air with fumes. The dreadful squawling outside gradually diminished and finally died out.

"It's worked!" I shouted triumphantly.

"Sure," Keega conceded.

We examined our injuries. Blood oozed from the ugly wounds, scratches and bruises. Major Keega had a bad cut on the forehead and

97

scratches above the right eye and arms. Our clothes were tattered.

We performed first aid on each other and dressed the wounds. We changed into clean attire.

"Could we investigate what happened?" I suggested.

"Yes, indeed."

The air outside was foul. The carrions looked like they had been there for ages. The surrounding grass appeared longer.

The decomposition process duly completed only left ghastly fur.

Gloria Gallows and Chattel Kamali intensified their hostility towards us. The sumptuous meals we had known in the Mausoleum vanished. In their place we were served execrable dishes that we ate out of extreme hunger. They left our bowels rumbling with flatulence. The water turned bitter.

The Mausoleum, once so spick and span, became more and more squalid. A repugnant stench filled the place. Whatever we did to keep the place clean was sabotaged. The walls cracked and became discoloured. The ceiling sagged in the some places. Before long, we were sharing the Mausoleum with strange insects and beasts like ants, cockroaches, snakes and mice. The only thing that seemed to improve was the quality of the effectiveness of the various intoxicating drinks and narcotics readily available here. The language adopted by the two slatternly women was vulgar, blasphemous and outright abusive. To increase our misery, the town sluts enhanced their indulgence in orgiastic rituals, sorcery and witchcraft. Once, during a conflict, Gloria Gallows transformed herself into a serpent. A huge dirty-brown serpent with seven massive heads. The forked tongues emitted a venomous spectrum. Their lidless eyes sparkled mesmerically. We narrowly escaped and remained locked up in 'Sojourn', as we had renamed Keega's bedroom, for three days without food or water.

On her part, Kamali had converted herself into a werewolf and hounded us day and night.

The conflict had sprung up from our objection to the maids' nocturnal visits to our bedrooms. We would be startled awake, to find the two nymphomaniacs ravishing us. In their frenzy, they would bite and tear at us with their nails, making horrid sounds. The sight of blood and our anguished cries gave them utmost enjoyment.

The perversive activities in the 'Confessional' increased both in frequency and intensity. They left both Keega and I in a state of deep

98

remorse and moral repugnance.

Gloria and Kamali had nocturnal friends. These friends brought with them virgins on whom they practised wild sexual torture.

They would dress them in burning rubber and then force them to lie on beds with electric needles. They would draw blood from them with knives and lances, assault them sexually and burn their remains when they finally died.

These experiences ultimately led to our disillusionment and change. We quit drinking. Gave up smoking. Disdained irresponsible sex and abstained from it. We derived whatever little joy and comfort we could from our solitude and meditations. We made every possible effort to remain calm in the face of adversity. To be bold and unshakable in turbulent situations.

The Creation, on its part, consoled and assured us that all this hell would be over, soon.

Chapter Fifteen

Satan suddenly returned from his mysterious mission.

"Hi, men," he greeted us cheerfully.

"Hello, sir," Keega and I replied, giving him aggrieved looks.

The sovereign sat on his Hot-seat. Majestic. Charming. Cajoling. Shortly, we had regaled him with our tales of woe in the Mausoleum during his absence. He listened in fascination, or so we thought. Then he laughed. A long mordant laughter.

"Most interesting, uh?"

We were stunned.

"I see you haven't been without adventure."

"Adventure?" we chorused, chagrined.

"Well, Kimuri, what would you term it?"

"Torture," I fumed.

"Keega?"

"Hell!"

"Okay, okay, now relax," he said, giving us a wry smile.

"We waited to see what other mysteries he had in store for us.

"So now, fellows," he continued confidently, "I'll let you in on a few secrets. Ultimately, you'll have the power to cope with any forces working against your interests."

We re-arranged the parlour. One wall would serve as a screen for slides and film-stripes to aid our understanding. These would highlight illustrations, diagrams, maps and statistical data.

We spent the whole morning learning how to learn effectively. How to understand human nature. Measurement and evaluation. Man's abilities and limitations.

"The most important pre-requisite in any learning situation," Satan counselled, "is will. Indomitable will to succeed."

We learnt how to attain the highest level of the conscious and the subconscious. Transcendental meditations. Hypnotism and voodooism.

We found the whole exercise most absorbing, totally different from our mundane systems of education which largely involved conditioning, introduction, and impractical theories and hypotheses.

We asked questions and we got answers. We performed experiments and empirically arrived at the truth. Satan took no umbrage at our ignorance and slow pace of absorption.

Time moves swiftly. Presently, lunch was served. The most delicious meal we had had for a long time. We ate voraciously. The dirges had now been replaced by martial music. We were exulted.

Satan had introduced us to new models of the arts and sciences of life. We could collude with all kinds of spirits. We could arrive at reality through the abstract. We could gasp both the visible and invisible realities easily. By invoking some spirits, we could divine future events through mathematical manoeuvres, observing smoke, communicating with men's souls and by necromancy.

We resumed our learning after lunch. Satan elucidated the principles of levitation. With the use of our supernormal powers, we could levitate long distances without the aid of machines, or balloons. We had only to direct our energies toward certain faculties within our system and then we could be lifted above the ground.

With the application of principles of reality through the abstract, we could make ourselves invisible. This, in effect, would enable us to contend with invisible spirits. We could quite easily recognize the various spirits we encountered, be they air, water, land or forest spirits.

These lessons took us far into the night. We had never had a more intriguing day, albeit arduous. By supper time, we were capable of seeing through a vista of years into the future. This, however, could not enable us to alter our fate. We could also fathom into the deepest secrets of the minds of other people, thereby deducing their intentions, fears, desires, hopes and attitudes towards different things. We could transmit thought waves and influence the other person to think or act as we desired.

Without the aid of translating machines or interpreters, we could address mammoth gatherings in only one language or through telepathy. "I feel great!" Keega boasted.

"Me, too."

"You are good learners," Satan remarked.

"Thank you, sir," we acknowledged.

"Be with you later, men."

He vanished.

We locked ourselves in 'Sojourn.' Still enthusiastic, we set the paraphernalia to work. The future intrinsically intrigued us.

Taking a foolscap and a pen, I scribbled the heading: FORECAST.

The first few experiments were simple and gave us obvious results. People on Earth are inescapably moving closer to the brotherhood of men.

Consequently, men will feel at home even in foreign countries, regardless of their birth-place, political inclinations or personal prejudices. Simply; they are moving towards the realization of world consciousness.

Struggle for power and material accumulation will always lead to war of one class of people against another. The haves and the have-nots. The old and the youth.

The ignorant and the literate. Men and women. The endeavours to redress the situation will always meet resistance and repression.

More labour-saving devices will be contrived. This will result in too much leisure. Inactivity will result in boredom. To curb it, people will indulge in licentious activities, most of which will culminate in various forms of suicide. This will affect even children.

Unemployment will mount. To cope with the escalating cost of living, pseudo-legal trade empires shall flourish side by side with the legal establishments. Ignorant and innocent citizens will inevitably find themselves caught up in the intricate network of organized crime.

There will be more medical and scientific break-throughs aimed at curing diseases and prolonging life-expectancy. But machine-imposed deaths will rise to confounding proportions. Motor vehicle, industrial and nuclear accidents will also abound.

Men, women and their progeny will be more and more automated. They will act like robots. They will depend more on drugs to suppress the harsh realities of life.

Commercial firms will spring up to provide diversions. In the long-run even these diversions will be taken to a point of addiction. Then, leisure will be just too expensive.

Moral values will disintegrate with time, giving way to selfishness and barbarism. Hardly will there be time to seriously consider anyone else. The marriage institution will be highly commercialized and adulterated. Marriage will be for the convenience of both or just one of the spouses. In most cases, it shall be sustained only to avoid adverse public opinion or for the children's sake.

Fear of truth will persist. Even the slightest element of truth will be politicized, hence, provocative. Truth shall be christened 'Classified Information', 'Confidential', 'Official Secrets'.

Privacy shall be a thing of the past. With the decline of privacy, personal liberty and security will diminish.

There will be scores of files and micro-data stored in computers on everyone. School records, insurance policies, bank accounts, income tax, employers records, hire purchase companies. Gossip and rumours, will be stored in data banks.

Human spare-parts will be sold in shops, established and licenced for this purpose. The catalogue might include: hearts, kidneys, testicles, limbs, blood and grafting skin.

Ways and means of inspecting the entire body for symptoms of suspected maladies will be improvised. Blood purification will be done by machines, at a price. Deformities will be corrected or concealed with aid of artificial devices or fashions.

In spite of family planning and the sterilization of men and women, world population will always explode; and especially in poorer and developing nations. Problems such as housing, crime, disease, lack of educational facilities, prostitution and poverty will prevail.

Where man succeeds in solving his old problems, there will always be new problems for him to grapple with. Over and above all, man's greatest challenge shall be in the management of his own affairs. Despite all these technological marvels and wonderful achievements, man will still be unable to attain the halcyon days of his ancestors.

We sat up late into the night, burning paper, bones, wood, clothes, and other articles to discern the hidden secrets. We used mathematical calculations. Delved in libations, abracadabra, invoked the obscene whispers of various spirits and recorded their revelations.

It was very late when we finally folded our papers and decided to go to sleep.

Chapter Sixteen

Events in Gehenna developed at an accelerated pace. Great multitudes gathered in every town the Creation was scheduled to conduct its anti-Satan campaigns. Eager and expectant. Our arrival was always heralded by supernatural phenomena like thunder, lightning, smoke and a great surge of voices. There were, among the masses, people convinced we were gods who could save them from the turmoil in which they had been inevitably caught. They defied us despite our protestations.

Teams of traditional dancers, choirs and dramatists performed. In their songs and poems, they lauded the Creation's achievements in man's struggle for liberty and human dignity. They invited more people to come forward and fight for their rights.

Placard carrying and slogan chanting youths marched before the rostrum on which the Creation's leaders were seated. One little girl carried a placard with a poem against Satan:

> *His reasoning is brilliant*
> *His plans ingenious*
> *His logic well-nigh irrefutable*
> *Prince of lofty stature*
> *Of unlimited craft and cunning*
> *Able to take advantage of every*
> *opportunity that presents itself*
> *Able to turn every situation*
> *to his own advantage.*

People then settled down.

We greeted them in various fashions, just to be sure we were on the same wave-length.

One very satisfying thing was that we addressed the gathering in only one language and they all understood our message without any difficult. We informed the audience the aims and objectives of the Creation. To promote universal peace and understanding among peoples of all nations regardless of their race, religion, sex or status; to arouse peoples' awareness to the issues of the times with a view to finding viable solutions and avert disasters which could easily result if these issues were neglected.

104

Among the issues we cited were the arms-race, population explosion, environmental pollution, education, health care, poverty and human rights and peoples' right to determine their destiny.

The new dynamic leader of the Creation, Neutron Godman, was invited to address the people.

Godman had a forceful personality. He radiated an aura of peace and enthusiasm. He was a founder member of the Creation and quite clearly understood what the movement stood for. He was a social scientist with many talents that he utilized fully. He was an author, journalist, educationalist-cum-evangelist.

In conferences, he talked confidently. He debated, argued and supported his view with pertinent information and cogent reasons.

"Dear friends," he began, "we all realize the important task we have set ourselves; to make our present worthwhile and our future fulfilling."

Mummers of approval.

"It is gratifying to observe that we all appreciate our various roles in the Creation's development programmes. You are not merely contented with the blarney of your politicians and religious demagogues."

Pause. He slowly surveyed the crowd and continued.

"We all have a duty. Every one of us! To strive for reform. To change for the better. To make your immediate environment a better place for yourself and all the others who dwell therein."

A tumultuous applause.

"The reform should begin with each individual cultivating peaceful thoughts. Be at peace with all and sundry."

"Peace ... peace! ... peace! ..." the multitude passionately chanted as if in prayer.

"Each individual extending warmth, love, understanding and recognition. Let your love flow to your neighbour, to the stranger, through nations to saturate the entire universe."

People joined hands and prayed. Mellowed with love. Acceptance!

"God is love, God is love ... If I don't love my neighbour I can't reach God. Love, peace, justice and mercy. Let us all divest ourselves of our conceit and selfishness. Let's be always prepared to make sacrifices for the benefit of others."

"Yes ... yes, indeed."

"Brethren, we have simply been floundering through life. Our exis-

105

tence has become a living-hell, seeking escape from reality, truth and from ourselves. In alcohol, narcotics and perversity. Enough!"

"Enough!" the crowd echoed. "Enough!" Alcoholics, drug addicts and perverts broke down in tears of mortification. "Man must live in peace. In dignity. We must learn to work without exploiting others. Let everybody participate in the political, economic and social life of the society.

"We should all aspire for peaceful co-existence, assert our right to determine our destiny and aim at positive achievements in all spheres of life."

The throng applauded.

"Now, comrades, the Creation is very grateful to the people who have been involved in our various endeavours. The youth organizations, student bodies, women groups, organizations and individuals who have tirelessly continued to support us in many, many ways."

Claps and ululations.

"Through their concerted efforts, we have successfully halted desertification through tree-planting programmes. Through their agricultural efforts and research, we have curbed malnutrition and famine. We have even managed to replenish our food reserves and to export the surplus. Through our efforts, we have been able to arrest soil erosion and reclaim swamps for agricultural purposes. We have cleaned our environment and improved our educational standards. To all these, good people, I say bravo!"

The crowd cheered.

"Good. Ladies and gentlemen, we are capable of many more stupendous achievements. But our enemy, Satan, is a formidable force! For eons, he has continued to exert baleful influence in all our affairs. We must vanquish him. With your support, of course. Extradite him to the Earth to be tried for the atrocities he and his ilk have perpetrated against mankind. The World Supreme Court of peace and justice shall ably handle this case. Our earnest endeavour is harmony, security, liberty and to promote human welfare to the heavenly realms. Thank you."

The ensuing applause was deafening.

It was now the Pope's turn to address the gathering.

"Leaders," the loud-speaker blared, "should set good examples. Examples that can be emulated by others. A leader should be a person fully committed to the welfare of his community. But, from our observations,

106

from the records of events, most leaders leave a lot to be desired. Many of them are corrupt and hypocritical. Sly manipulators of people and events."

The pontiff paused and cleared his throat. He was a short stout man with chubby cheeks, shrewd eyes and an effeminately shrill voice. On his chest he wore an enormous gold crucifix. His mouth was crammed with gold teeth.

Pope Peace-Love I. He had changed his names from Pope Rob Driftsham I. A man wholly committed to the Creation's cause for humanity.

The open-air mass at Mammon Square in Badtown was attended by the biggest crowd ever seen in the city.

"I have met leaders who condemn tribalism. Yet, they practise it in their choice of senior officers. Leaders who, wearing sanctimonious masks, profess justice, yet they manipulate the organs of the judiciary for their own interests. Leaders who run the affairs of their states like private enterprises. National resources are used for personal enrichment and consolidation of power. Leaders who employ military might to intimidate and repress the citizens. Leaders who use oppressive means to suppress criticism and dissent."

He coughed again. Violently.

"Millions of people starve. Millions more go homeless. Many strong and intelligent people remain jobless, while the powerful and the affluent hold several jobs. We've held talks with most of these leaders. We've clearly explained to them the Creation's stand in these matters. They must change! Change and adopt more utilitarian policies for the good of the majority they lead."

"There are also some among you leaders, religious leaders, who are lethargic, if not altogether apathetic to crucial issues regarding the welfare of mankind and their spiritual development. These religious prostitutes are even ready to compromise their spiritual well-being for material and political rewards. They betray the the church of God. They lead many innocent people to unnecessary suffering. They endorse exploitation. They condone larceny. They uphold immorality and promote racial discrimination. We have very many examples in Dunia, Cannibia, Ghasia and other states of Gehenna. We, religious leaders, have a duty to re-educate the masses. Enlighten them on their God-given rights that are inalienable. Caution them openly. Frankly. Even in matters of sex and family life. Sex

107

is one of the noblest endowments in most living beings. Yet sex is most misunderstood and repressed. It has contributed immensely to break-downs in moral, psychological and physical make-ups. It has become a merchandise to be sold, advertised and promoted in films, televisions, radio, newspapers and magazines.

"I therefore, appeal to all religious leaders to re-dedicate themselves to God. Re-examine themselves, repent and pray for forgiveness.

"Beware of succumbing to despondency. Likewise, beware of mun-dane pleasures that might divert you from the truth. But, above all, eschew evil from among you. Extirpate greed and violence from your midst and strive for peace, justice, unity of purpose and security for all. We should transcend fear and suffering, and even death. Let all people of good-will join hands with the Creation to overcome evil with good. Conquer Satan and build a better world."

The congregation then joined in prayer. As they prayed for forgive-ness, courage, reconciliation, faith and healing, they witnessed many miracles. The blind saw. The deaf heard. The dumb talked. Families were reunited in love and reconciliation. People were, in effect, inspired to realize their optimum potentials and to share liberally.

Sermons were distributed as the congregation dispersed.

The struggle continued.

We persisted in propagating our gospel of peace, love, justice, unity and progress. Major Keega and I felt party to the conspiracy. We were duty-bound to the oath to which we first joined the Creation. At the same time, there was a sense of adventure and the thrill of danger.

Our intensive training in intelligence and military skills made our work immensely enjoyable. We continued to work closely with Marshall Pendo, who had duly changed his name from Marshall Gikuu.

The Creation had successfully reasoned with some statesmen. Some accepted to institute changes in their governments. To improve on their human rights records, and the quality of life of their citizens. They convinced their people of the need for change of attitude. To become less self-seeking. To work towards noble goals such as unity, increased food-production, education, elimination of poverty, creating employment and training opportunities.

But, some of the robber barons , drug-traffickers, arms-dealers and perpetrators of other anti-social activities were vexed. They did everything in their power to defeat the Creation's efforts.

They instigated arrests of our members. Most of them were tortured, constrained to sign confessions to implicate them in fabricated charges.

Some of the heads of states who were sympathetic with the Creation were assassinated. Other members just vanished mysteriously.

People realized the amount of power they possessed. Power that enabled them to oust some despotic and corrupt regimes; replacing them with more democratic, community-centered governments. Among the leaders ousted were those dogged by scandals: Financial scandals, sex scandals, graft scandals, murder scandals, drug-running and military bribery scandals.

In numerous cases, the army toppled dictators and handed the government to the people.

But all was not smooth-sailing for us. Our work met with suspicion, resistance and mixed feelings. All this clearly indicated man's obduracy to change. Rowdy mobs disrupted our rallies in some cities. Attempts were made on our lives. We received warnings, threats, and letter bombs.

Pope Peace-Love I sustained serious injuries, while several people died when unknown assailants attacked him with chemical weapons in a crowded meeting in Ghasia. The rostrum was completely destroyed. Some youths were apprehended. They confessed. They had been hired to assassinate members of the Creation.

These hostile reactions were fuelled by our success in educating the masses.

Clergymen loyal to the Creation's ideals were harassed by State Security personnel in their endeavour to intimidate them from propagating the truth. Church members were persecuted. Our newspapers, the *Conscience*, *Truth* and *Exposé* were banned. Their chief offence was that they exposed corruption in high places. They had exposed episodes of favouritism, exploitation and hypocrisy.

But our bitterest enemies were people who enriched themselves through slavery, fraud and trade in harmful and addictive drugs. People with no qualms or conscience about the number of lives they snuffed out; the victims they permanently maimed; and the families they orphaned through their activities in their pursuit of wealth and power.

In every state of Gehenna, there were saboteurs paid to see that we did not succeed in our endeavours. Marauding terrorists went round hurling chemical bombs, petrol, bottles and stones on suspected Creation members. Mysterious accidents took toll of our supporters, both on the roads and in factories. Anarchists led in demonstrations and protests against any form of authority. In Badtown, they lured school girls into prostitution and male student into crime.

Before long, one factor rose against another. Disunity became a vital weapon. Opportunism among Creation members led some to betray our cause. While coming from an urgent session in Shamblesville to seek ways and means of resolving these crises, Keega and I were besieged by a team of policemen, all heavily armed. We were escorted to Purgatory Maximum Security Prison where we were detained.

CHAPTER SEVENTEEN

Life in prison was hell. Inhuman! There were brutal, frustrated, semi-literate, poorly-paid warders venting their frustrations and vengeance on the damned. There was a strange assortment of prisoners too: political prisoners who had fallen from grace with their systems; dignified, self-assured and respectable looking lawyers, academics and students who had opted to suffer rather than sell their conscience. These were contemptuously referred to as dissidents, rebels, revolutionaries, enemies of the people and misguided elements.

Some people just found themselves inevitably where they were. Nowhere! Some had only a vague notion of reasons behind their incarceration: suspicious conduct, crimes of thought, criticism of oppressive regimes and possession of information they were not supposed to know.

There were also true, incorrigible criminals boasting unbeatable records of crimes like murder, assault, rape, treason, espionage, robbery with violence, terrorism and sedition. The majority of prisoners chose to live nostalgically in their glorious past rather than live in the doomed present and uncertain future.

Often in conversation one heard:

"When I was a Minister ..."

"Once I was a police boss ..."

"I had the most wonderful family. ... then one day I got very annoyed. I massacred everyone and drank poison."

"I used to be the most affluent and successful business tycoon in my area. Then my fortunes changed. For worse!"

"If I were to live my live all over again ..."

At first we were utterly confounded. We were not quite certain we were in jail, a human butchery or a mental institution. There were formidable armed guards rasping harsh orders and curses, beating up inmates with barbed whips, truncheons, and gun-butts. Some to death.

The tougher ones fought back. A fellow called Buster killed one of the burly guards and devoured his brains. The incensed guards teamed up and battered the culprit to pulp.

Lunatics screamed and yelled their heads off. The violent ones fought among themselves or molested other inmates. Others were pre-occupied

111

with eating dirt and the waste matter in the squalid cell.

The condition in the cell was aggravated by drunkards who got sick and vomited and urinated carelessly. The cell reverberated with curses, screams and groaning of people in agony. Some from injuries sustained by police torture during the interrogation and others from being urinated or defecated on.

I noted with horror that in connivance with the guards, some prisoners were able to smuggle in drugs and weapons with which they committed murder or suicide. The guards traded in pornographic photographs, cigarettes and narcotics and made arrangements for sexual encounters. Letters and other forms of messages would also be smuggled out with a bribe.

My crutches were already beginning to feel heavy and burdensome. My tongue impulsively kept on exploring the gaps in my mouth where I had lost several teeth during the interrogation. The multiple burns and razor-cuts on my flesh hurt terribly. My entire body felt paralyzed from the beating and the electric shocks.

Major Keega groaned on one side near the wall. They had worked on him till he could not move a limb. He had to be confined to a wheel-chair. His whole body was swathed in bloody bandages.

We had witnessed people die under police brutality. Some were shot in cold blood. Others were forced to make false self-incriminating confessions, hoping to extenuate their suffering. Perhaps we were only saved by the fact that we were what the police boss had called V.I.Ps. That is Very Important Prisoners.

We lost our belongings at the police station. Our special watches, photographs, notes, pens and wallets.

The congestion, the oppressive heat, offensive odours and the abnormal and shameful activities of the wardens and the inmates in the grisly cell made life unbearable.

Things moved from bad to worse. Keega and I were condemned to solitary confinement. In Limbo and Utopia respectively. I was hurled into Utopia, a mysterious dungeon. The intense darkness lasciviously devoured me.

"Let me out! Save me, please!" I wailed, exasperated. "Help! He–l–p! Get me out of here pl–e–a–se!"

Nothing happened. I became angry. Bitter. Vindictive. Had they left me here to die? What was their plan? To drive me crazy? What chances

112

were there for my survival? Escape?

I groped in the dark trying to feel the walls. Apparently there were no walls. No ceiling. Just an infinite expanse of emptiness. The hard floor felt chilling and dank. It was slimy in places.

I was stark naked.

The ominous silence was terrible. Terrible. The pounding of my heart sounded like a drum. My breathing was like the noises made by bellows.

Since our incarceration in Purgatory Maximum Security Prison, we had been denied food, water and medical attention. So far we had hardly slept. The authorities had only been kind enough to douse us with drugs that left us utterly debilitated and feeling completely disoriented. Now, in Utopia, I could not cope with the monotony of. The boredom. The solitude. The inability to think and act. I could not distinguish day from night. Night from day. I existed in eternity. In oblivion, traversing the infinite space and slithering on the slimy floor. I only managed to hurt myself in a bid to commit suicide.

Finally, utterly exhausted, I collapsed and willed death.

> *Death,*
> *O, Sweet Death,*
> *Kindly take heed*
> *And come to my aid*
> *In the hour of my direct need.*

Amid tight security, Keega and I were escorted before a Judicial Commission of Inquiry for another gruelling interrogation.

The commission was presided over by the most awe inspiring judge of the supreme court. These included the Chief Justice Savage, Mr. Justice Reverse, Justice Lady (Mrs.) Man, Mrs. Justice Masimango and Mr. Justice Denial.

Other officials included grave, bald-headed, and be-spectacled professionals, inter alia: judges, psychiatrists, psychologists and neurologists. Some of them smoked incessantly. Others probed us with seering gazes. They all affected stony, expressionless faces.

Among the allegations levelled against us were:

One; we belonged to a covert organization called Creation whose interests and operations were not in the best interest of the Kingdom of Gehenna.

113

Two; we had behaved in a manner prejudicial to the interests and perpetuation of the Kingdom of Satan.

Three; we had been involved in conspiracies to demolish the influences of Satan and the good government of Gehenna by unlawful means.

Four; we had been party to convening unlawful meetings to recruit new members and propagate acrimonious ideologies foreign and unacceptable in Gehenna.

Five; we had acquired sophisticated ultra-modern arms and trained personnel in a bid to topple Satan and destroy the Kingdom of Gehenna.

As the prosecutor rasped the various indictments in a harsh voice, Keega and I re-appraised each other compassionately. Both of us were ill, emaciated, haunted and bedraggled in prison garb.

At the mention of 'sophisticated ultra-modern arms, I suddenly realized, with shock, how man often forgets to use his best faculties in an emergency. We had completely forgotten our special powers which we could have used against our adversaries and avoided all this suffering. I communicated with Major Keega through telepathy.

The account of our experiences in Gehenna as contained in our disquisitions was examined and cross-examined. We protested against detention without trial, torture of prisoners in the hands of police and prison authorities and the abhorrent conditions in jail, which succeeded more in dehumanizing prisoners than rehabilitating them.

We decried indiscipline among the security forces and objected to the shooting of suspects. We condemned the humiliation, degradation, oppression and exploitation of prisoners and all forms of human rights abuse.

Ultimately, the verdict was brought in. Guilty. Keega and I were condemned to imprisonment for seven lives each, in Purgatory Maximum Security Prison. In solitary confinement.

The verdict galvanized us into action.

As the security men approached to hustle us to perdition, a strange power filled us. We fought viciously and subdued our armed captors.

Explosions reverberated throughout the court precincts.

Reinforcements rushed in. We swiftly made ourselves invisible, levitated into the air and made our exit through the doors, left open in the rush and confusion.

We found the others in Future House, an ultra-modern edifice with

114

sensitive walls that transmitted photographs and messages immediately one approached.

"And here they are," Dr. Felicitous Web announced, even before we had become visible.

"Oh, great! exclaimed Neutron Godman. "This is simply wonderful."

"Yeah," agreed Marshal Pendo, "We should be able to go on with our plans. Three days to zero hour A.D. 2052."

"Precisely," Godman concurred.

"Welcome, gentlemen. We were really worried about you. Our medium, Dr. Felicitous Web, kept us informed about your tribulations in Purgatory. Attempts had been made to reach you but to no avail."

"Thank you, ladies and gentlemen, for your concerted efforts. It's a miracle that we're here," I said gratefully.

We regaled them with the details of the trial, the verdict and our escape. "Sure, sure," they conceded. "It's a miracle."

"And you know what, gentlemen," Marshal Pendo volunteered, "We were able to recover your watches and cameras. The police officers who had confiscated them from you wanted to keep them for themselves. They suddenly died mysteriously. Our men followed the signals and recovered the articles."

"Thank you, sir" Major Keega acknowledged. "We really appreciate your efforts."

The transcendental music in the house had a healing effect to the soul. In another room, we were pathologically examined on computer beds. Our various maladies were treated. Our blood was de-toxified. After bathing and having a gargantuan meal, we slept.

We woke up later, sparkling with good health.

CHAPTER EIGHTEEN

Chaos and anarchy reigned over Gehenna. Everything suddenly went topsy-turvy. Disaster after disaster struck. Numberless grisly accidents annihilated human resources, maimed many and let others and their dependants destitutes. Intractable wars erupted among the states. Chemical weapons and other unconventional ballistic missiles were employed. Widespread robberies plagued both the government and private organizations. The most nuisance were by thieves armed with pens, computers, legality and in most cases, holding most responsible and enviable positions. Arson, looting, terrorism and other forms of senseless violence swept over the cities and the countryside. Unbridled sexual promiscuity and perversion resulted in mysterious, incurable and highly infectious diseases that spread like bush fire, affecting even the unborn. Drunkenness and alcoholism was superceded by escalating use of narcotics, especially among the youth. Prices of commodities escalated. Inflation got out of control. Workers and low-cadre business entrepreneurs groaned in their misery and poverty. Cannibalism and exploitation led to graft, smuggling, bribery and corruption. Energy crises became endemic. People became slaves to machines. Science repressed humanity. Armies were cloned in the laboratory and despatched to war. Areas previously affected by famine because of drought experienced unusually heavy acid rains. People died in acid floods, from starvation, pestilences, earthquakes and lightning. Volcanoes previously dormant, erupted. Whole cities and villages perished.

The Creation's forces worked assiduously. Units with food aid, medicine supplies and equipment were dispatched to the worst hit regions. The parties comprised medical personnel, experts, students, the fire-brigade and social workers.

Our surveillance and reconnaissance satellites signalled false alarms. Our programmed missiles and rockets were automatically activated. Nuclear disasters spread unabated. I recalled Pope Peace-Love I's scriptural reference in our last All Religious Prayers Fellowship:

> *Put on the armour of God*
> *So that you can stand the Devil's Schemes*
> *For our struggle is not against the flesh and*
> *   blood*

But against the rulers
Against the authorities
Against the powers of this dark world
And against the spiritual forces of evil
     in the Heavenly realms.

Therefore, put on the full armour of God
So that when the day of evil comes
You may be able to stand your ground
And after you have done everything
To stand

The words spoken to us by Satan kept repeating themselves in my mind:

"There are other departments where we have machines programmed to register and regulate natural phenomena like the change of weather in the entire Kingdom of Gehenna."

I remembered even having asked him what he could do after receiving the alarm in Vigilante.

"Set Hell loose."

So that was it. *Hell loose*!

Now! the signal came. The Mausoleum was besieged. Deliverance, Uhuru, Salvation and Utamaduni battalions were alert, their sophisticated armoured crafts, *Life, Discipline* and *Vision* set.

Move!

My troop raced across the ground to Satan's domicile. While the other soldiers burst into the complex, Major Keega and I sprung up to the Seventh floor.

Working frantically, we deactivated the robots and immobilized Satan's military and surveillance facilities, using special equipment and Laser guns.

Wearing gas-masks, our accessories — ethics, morals and love ready, we searched frantically from room to room. The kitchen, the Confessional, Laboratory and Vigilante. Satan was nowhere!

"The Parlour!" Major Keega argued.

The 'Hot Seat' was there, blazing sprightly. Martial music filled the air. But Satan wasn't there!

We gassed the room. Objects started to explode.

We raced to our former bedrooms and rummaged through the wardrobes. We packed our best suits, the jewels left behind by Waruo and Zawadi — gold, silver and diamonds and all the pictures we had taken in Gehenna, notes, micro-tapes and cassettes.

As we dashed through the corridor, we crashed into Gloria Gallows and Chattel Kamali. We fell with our paraphernalia flying into the air, landing several metres away.

"Where's Satan?" I demanded from Gloria, ignoring my bleeding nose and lower lip.

"Not here. What's all this?" Gloria countered.

"A coup!" Keega bawled at them.

The two maids sprung on us like tigers.

"You can't get away!" Kamali hissed.

We fought, wildly tearing at each other. Gloria Gallows used her sharp nails, teeth and her forehead to try to subdue me.

I suddenly kicked her in the crotch, and at the same time dived for my laser gun. Before she could rise up, I vapourized her.

Keega vanquished Kamali just as I was about to go to his aid.

"Demons," Keega remarked.

"Where's the Devil?" I enquired.

"Possibly among our men."

A mysterious fire crackled triumphantly, consuming everything in its way. Smoke and flames curled viciously upwards forming ugly dark clouds.

The roof fell in. Presently, Satan's domicile—The Mausoleum—was a mass of fire. Horrified screams rent the air. While our attention was riveted on the fire, strange creatures emerged from the shadows and killed some of our soldiers. There were terrible noises everywhere. A fierce battle ensued.

"Retreat!" Marshal Pendo issued the order.

We shot at our adversaries while retreating towards our crafts, but the apparitions followed us, undaunted.

Then Satan's mordant voice filled the air:

"You human beings are never satisfied. You never see what you have. But instead always see what you desire to have. No wonder you have never attained lasting happiness and peace in your miserable lives."

118

He paused. Everything was petrified. Everything stood still. I was stunned.

"Man does not achieve anything durable socially, politically, economically, even spiritually because of greed, folly and egoism."

The atmosphere became chilly. Satan continued. "You lack patriotism for your world. Extolling nationalism and racism. You maul one another and blame Satan. Where is your wit, oh man? How practical is the Utopia you seek to build without changing your attitude towards your fellow man?

"I've been amused by your gospel of love and justice while you continue to oppress the poor, amass wealth and pursue artificial values, while treading on human lives.

"You wage senseless wars, create veritable hells on Earth and blame Satan for this. The truth is: there are worse Satans in men than I, Lucifer, the Sovereign of Gehenna."

At this juncture, some missiles exploded.

"Of course, I know you are still armed, but note: No human-devised weapons, no matter how ingenious, can harm me. I'm beyond human handling," he rasped angrily. "And, that you may know that I am Satan Lucifer who fought with God Almighty over the dominion of the Heavenly realms, you will all perish!"

We were all visibly trembling with fear. Suddenly, Dr. Felicitous Web again began whimpering. Her perennial beauty withered. Her face was all wrinkled with age. Her figure shrank. Just as it had been with Zawadi, in the Confessional.

Satan's army started to advance upon us. Mechanically. Apparently enjoying every moment of our terror, despair and utter helplessness. We shot at the eerie creatures, frantically. All in vain. Shadows began to swoop above us — from all directions.

Juvenile Kijana shot himself through the mouth. Professor Femines Tabasamu tried to do the same but Marshal Pendo kicked the laser gun from her hand.

The next moment, we were madly scurrying away from the Evil Forces of Satan. They gave chase, spluttering and making all sorts of horrid noises. We ran on. Yet, the heavy breathing and throaty noises of our pursuers followed.

Tree branches lashed at us. Nettles stung. Thorns bruised us. Weird animals, robots, zombies and insects were all set against us.

My colleagues were out-distancing me. I accelerated, but all in vain. My lungs were bursting. Eventually, I came to a cave. Taking little consideration that there might be vampires or snakes, I plunged into the dark cave.

With a lot of difficulty, I pressed forward like a troglodyte, gradually getting used to the darkness. The demoniacal noises behind me kept getting closer, closer, closer ...

I stumbled and fell. I scrambled up and scuttled on. Each time I paused to listen, the noise would still be nearby. Just as I was beginning to lose hope, I saw a glimmer of light in the distance. I struggled to reach it. Suddenly, I fell flat on my belly in a stream inside the cave. The cold water refreshed me momentarily. I picked myself up and trudged on.

Ultimately, I managed to reach the spiralling hymen of light, violently perforating it with my head. I found myself in a more spacious world, full of fresh air, light and a motley of colours.

I was trying to regulate my breathing when suddenly, a shadow crossed my path. The whole multitude of demons was descending upon me, Satan among them! I dashed for cover under the cruel bushes and dodged my way in haste.

The next moment I glanced behind me, Satan was gaining ground on me. Fire and smoke issued intermittently from his mouth and nostrils. He was reaching out for me with his bloody talons. I stumbled and fell, scraping flesh from my elbow and knees. I bled all over the body. I wished the ground would open up and swallow me alive. It didn't.

Before I could muster enough strength to spring back to my feet, Satan reached down for me. His deadly fangs sought my throat. His bloody claws sought my eyes, to gorge them out!

"Oh, my God!" I prayed, "Save me!"

Satan staggered and fell down with a terrible thud that shook the ground. I touched my neck. The crucifix that Pope Peace-Love I had put on my neck for protection was still there.

Satan was abruptly transformed into a cadaverous form of rotten flesh with fat wriggling maggots. The charred flesh vanished, leaving behind only bones, emitting phosphorescent light. From his rib-cage, a cobra, hissing frightfully, emerged. It started thrusting forward towards me, jutting out its baneful tongue. A spectrum of colours squirting from its venom. The serpent opened its enormous elastic jaws to devour me by the head. I jerked up with all my might in an endeavour to elude it. I found myself hurtling down through a fathomless abyss.

CHAPTER NINETEEN

I came to, amid sighs of relief. My eyelids felt extraordinarily heavy. My vision was blurred. My whole body felt strange.

I was propped up in bed with pillows. Drips fixed to my body. I was drenched in sweat like a racing horse.

"Kimuri," someone called me. But I wasn't quite sure. The voices seemed to be coming from a far distance.

"Oh, yes … yes … yes …" another voice said, "he's coming to."

"Hello, Kimuri," the first voice called again. "Can you hear me, Kimuri? If you do, please make a sign. Wink, slowly, up and down three times. Come on now, Kimuri …"

I did.

"Good," the first voice said. "Now he's past the danger."

"Yeah," agreed the second voice, "but he still needs a lot of rest. Instruct Rehema to make his ward arrangements."

Gradually, the faces around became more discernible. They were both masked. Despite the rubber masks, one of the figures had the features of Marshal Pendo. I gazed at him questioningly. Why was I dreaming of being in Gehenna while I was still on Earth or of being on Earth while I was still in Gehenna?

I looked around. We were in a room redolent with carbolic smells of the hospital. An electric tube hung over me. I was lying on a bed covered with white sheets. At the bedside table was an assortment of doctor's paraphernalia: stethoscopes, thermometers, chronometers, syringes, notes on clip-boards and small medicine-bottles.

The two doctors examined me closely.

Presently, the door opened gently and a nurse entered. I could not follow their conversation, but they all seemed delighted with their efforts. They were still conversing in low tones when I fell asleep.

I woke up in an entirely different room.

Three weeks elapsed. Sometimes it is astonishing how rapidly time fleets away. Tomorrows soon become yesterdays. Yesterdays with their memories. Good and bad. Yesterdays with unfulfilled desires and regrets.

I've heard it said that convalescence is the most abhorrent time for many

122

people, and especially those with painful maladies. Some people have defined the world during these circumstances as one interminable Hell. Maybe they are right. I don't know. My stay in Nyahururu District Hospital was quite different. The doctors, nurses and orderlies were ever friendly and considerate. Among my idols was Rehema, my ward-nurse. A tall beautiful lady with a trim figure. She was in her early twenties. Twenty-three at the most. She was ever immaculate in her white uniform. She always wore a sweet smile that went out to the patients like a good-will signal. I liked everything about Rehema — her patience, tolerance, sweet voice and charm.

At first, Rehema used to report to me whenever my relatives, friends and colleagues visited me. She would usher them into my ward and later tip them when the visiting hour was about to elapse. She assisted me in taking care of the presents they brought me, such as books, magazines and postcards.

Next to my father, the most frequent visitor to my ward was Bliss. We were drawn much closer to each other in my time of adversity. On her first visit, she had looked at me and cried shamelessly before she left. That we earnestly loved each other was beyond any doubt. She kept me well-informed about the latest developments in our place of work.

On one occasion she suddenly turned to me and said, "Darling, do you remember your colleague, Diehard Muhaini?"

"Of course, Love. Have I been away for so long that I should forget my work-mates?"

"He attempted suicide."

"What?" I gasped, horrified.

"Suicide," she continued. "The neighbours heard him groaning. On investigation, they found him in a deluge of vomit, urine and shit. Unconscious. The police rushed him to hospital. When he regained consciousness, he was a mad man. Jesus, he assaulted the doctor and wounded the nurse. He was over-powered and confined in a straight-jacket."

"Good God," I moaned, "What did the poor fool have to commit suicide for?"

"Can't tell," she shrugged her exquisite shoulders.

"Any suicide note?"

"Yes," she said, "The police found it in his jacket pocket. They haven't
123

yet disclosed its contents."

I sighed mournfully. "Really sad."

"Indeed. I'm wondering if our institution is not bewitched," Bliss observed solemnly.

Before she left, she kissed me and urged me to recover quickly so that we could get on with our plans.

Rehema came in with a conspiratorial smile. "You have a nice chick there. She's always asking after your health even long before coming in to see you."

"Thanks. That's why I'm so fond of her," I confessed, sincerely.

My father came in the next day. After enquiring after my health, he sighed. Then, with some difficulty, composed himself before he spoke.

"Son," he began, in a strained voice, "I have very sad news for you." He paused.

I waited patiently. I expected him to repeat Bliss' story about Muhaini's suicide bid. But what he said shocked me.

"It's about your friend, Keega."

"Mmh."

"The one who visited us last Christmas and we slaughtered a goat." I nodded.

"He's dead," my father said, slowly and paused as if to swallow a bitter lump.

Tears streamed down my cheeks frantically. I mourned without shame. I could regrettably envisage my friend, Keega, sprawled on a mortuary slab, dead. To make matters worse, here I was, helpless, propped up in a hospital bed. Why did it have to happen this way? Oh, God, why?

Apparently Bliss was right. Our institution was bewitched. I bit my lower lip so hard that it bled.

"What happened?" I enquired, turning to my father. He suddenly looked older, haggard and weak.

"Road accident. His car crashed into a truck near the River Engare Uasonyiro bridge. It was thrown over the bridge into the river. He was long dead before anyone could reach him."

I could vividly recall the afternoon Keega, Muhaini and I had had lunch at Heshima Restaurant and his jovial mood as he bid me farewell before driving off for Nairobi. Least did I suspect that that was the last time I would ever see him. He had even advised me to look out for my picture in his paper, *The Daily Mirror*, that week. And now this!

"I am profoundly shocked," I said.

"It's really sad," my father lamented. "The rate at which road accidents have increased is alarming. Yet, there is no way one can travel without using this means.

That morning, my father's visit was brief. After Rehema had emptied his bag of a packet of milk, fruits and the books he had brought me, he pressed my hand affectionately. A wave of emotion passed between us.

"Good-bye, my son."

"Good-bye, dear father."

Once alone, I lay on my back staring blankly at the white ceiling.

I reflected on my strange dream. I especially remembered how closely Keega and I had associated in Gehenna throughout our stay there. Right through to the battle against Satan. The Armageddon. It was during this battle that we had lost contact with each other.

That morning, I felt utterly confused. Not even Rehema could engage me in conversation. I preferred to be alone. To think.

This abrupt change in my temperament alarmed the nurse. Suspecting that I was relapsing, she informed Doctor Muganga and Doctor Vuyanzi. They promptly checked my pulse, temperature and breathing. I was alright. I needed rest.

In the afternoon, Nurse Rehema announced some unexpected visitors for me. Mr. Kiongo came in accompanied by some police officers. He introduced them as Inspector Tumaini, Corporals Haraka and Lengo. They asked questions about the afternoon I was rushed to hospital. My activities in the day and the people I has associated with. I answered them all to the best of my recollection. They recorded a statement.

The next group of visitors were pressmen from Keega's paper — The *Daily Mirror*. After the interview one took my photograph and they left.

I was discharged from the hospital and that was the greatest day in my life.

Relatives, friends and neighbours all came to congratulate me on my recovery. Mr. Kiongo, Bliss and her parents, Rehema, Doctor Muganga and Doctor Vuyanzi, Keega's parents and relatives were among the many guests. The occasion was also covered by the press.

"I'm glad that you'll soon be joining us. We have all missed you a lot during your illness. Only I won't be with you much longer," Mr Kiongo

125

said when we were left alone. He paused to gauge my reaction.

"Why?"

"Well," he shrugged, "I've been transferred to the headquarters in Nairobi." He pulled out a Khaki envelope from his coat pocket. It had a bold REPUBLIC OF KENYA inscription.

My heart was thumping wildly long before I had finished reading the letter.

"Incredible!" I exclaimed.

"Congratulations on your well-deserved promotion, Kimuri," Mr. Kiongo said, shaking my hand enthusiastically. "Now you are the Chief Agricultural Officer in Nyandarua. Best wishes. I'm sorry about your friend, Keega. He was a good chap."

Keega had been buried a week before I left hospital. His grandparents at Kamandura, Limuru had requested that he be buried on his father's land as he was the eldest and only son.

Mr. Kiongo also revealed that Diehard Muhaini had been transferred from Gilgil to Mathare Mental Hospital. He had grown extremely wild. He had lately injured other patients.

Police investigations conducted by Inspector Tumaini and his team had confirmed Muhaini's suicide note that he had poisoned Keega and I. They had interrogated the stewardess who had served us at Heshima Restaurant that afternoon.

She testified that she had witnessed Muhaini pouring something in our food from a small bottle which he had then returned into his coat pocket. The Government chemist had identified the drug as Pentox Parathion. Traces of the same drug were found in Keega's body during the postmortem.

The culprit had just returned from visiting farmers at Pondo Leshau when we picked him up on the way. He had all the drugs on him unknown to us. He got the chance to poison our food when I visited the toilets and my friend Keega, had gone out briefly to check on his car.

Muhaini had envied my rapid progress at work. But, then, why did the innocent Keega have to suffer? Just because he was my friend? That is the whole trouble of dealing with evil-minded people.

This was also a special occasion for Bliss. She had not visited me at home previously. My parents had only met Bliss several times sitting at the edge of my bed. I had introduced them.

Pastor Muhalellujah, who was a great family friend, delivered a short sermon on God's love for all of us. He said that God knew each one of us individually and our relationship with Him highly depended on our trust and obedience to Him.

"He is loving, understanding and merciful. Always ready to come to our aid when we cry to Him in prayer."

For the benefit of Keega's parents he said that we should learn to cope with the inevitable. He said that God knew before hand all that would happen to us and everything worked in accordance with His plan.

"Sometimes," the pastor continued, "calamities may befall us, as a lesson to us and others whom He wished to instruct through us."

"Consider the case of Job," he pointed out, "a God-fearing man of integrity. Yet he suffered all sorts of catastrophes."

The pastor advised that we should all endeavour to recognize our talents and put them to the best use. These various talents should be utilized in promotion of God's work in every sphere of life.

After a short thanks-giving prayer, we sat down for tea.

A wave of exhilaration surged through me as I walked towards our offices. Generally, everything seemed to be the same except for the new building which had now been completed. The faces and the flowers were all familiar. Everybody seemed only too eager to exchange greetings and a few platitudes with me. At one point I over-heard some two ladies talking.

"Yes, he's the one," one said.

"The one who had gone mad?" the other asked.

"I don't know if it was madness. But he was critically ill. It is even said that he shouted at boss — Mr. Kiongo."

"*Ngai*, then he must have been mad, how could he?"

At this juncture they looked up and saw me looking at them in amusement. They were embarrassed. I smiled at them then walked on.

People are curious! So word had already gone round even to the new employees that I was mad. And was I?

A debonair Mr. Kiongo cordially welcomed me to his office. We reviewed their achievements during my sick-leave.

He briefed me on my new responsibilities and benefits. I was entitled to a pay-rise, a higher house allowance and a car-loan.

He explained to me the circulars and programmes from the Ministry of Agriculture. There would be a staff-meeting that afternoon.

I felt wonderful to be among friends again. Time seemed to slip away imperceptibly. Presently, it was lunch time. Bliss waited for me in the sunshine outside.

"Darling, I've been wondering why anyone could wish you dead," Bliss began, as we sipped our soda after the food at Thomsons' Falls Lodge. "But after doing some hard thinking, I guess I now know."

"Come on, Sweetie, don't let it bother you any more."

"We can't dismiss it so easily, dear. You seem not to realize what you mean to me. And after all, truth is eternal, whether expressed verbally or repressed in the subconscious."

"Okay, Okay, Baby, let's hear it."

"Muhaini was a jealous man. He saw you as a great challenge to him. In all spheres of life where he had failed abysmally, you seemed to succeed with a minimum of effort."

"Yes …"

"He had other problems, too. He had miserably failed as a father and husband. His wife had eloped with one of his friends. The matter is still before the court."

"Yes?"

"He had twice applied for transfer. Each time he was unsuccessful. You've been promoted over him although he was older and more experienced than you are."

"Right."

"He had been keenly watching the development of our relationship with envy."

"Is that so?"

"Oh, yes. He once asked me for a date. I turned him down."

"Oh, but you've done it to me, too?"

"Well, but with you it was different. I didn't want to seem cheap. But here I am. You've got me. And I've got you."

"You're right," I admitted. "I see you've done your homework. I'm happy to be marrying a woman with brains."

"Thanks."

I pressed her hand gently and we both understood.

It wasn't until a few days later, after I had settled in my new office that I found myself trying to fathom my dream in the strange land of Gehenna.

128

A strong desire to record it came to my mind. I selected a clean leaf in my writing pad and started scribbling down my reflections.

Frankly speaking, I was amazed at some of the revelations in the dream. There also seemed to be something devine in it. God's power. The way He answers our prayers when we earnestly desire His help.

Despite Satan's pride that no human-devised weapon could harm him, the short extempore prayer I had uttered brought him tumbling down in all his might and sovereignty.

The experience had a profound effect on my life. I learnt to take life more seriously. To use my time, money and property more constructively in a way that could be beneficial, not only to myself, but to all those who deserve my assistance.

I also learned to respect and to be courteous to other people, regardless of their status, attitudes and reactions towards me. Consider their opinion, always maintaining a calm disposition, poise and a willingness to learn new lessons day by day.

Until now I had found it ludicrous to tell anyone, in detail, about this dream. I set to work, to put it down on paper. One thing I'll never understand though is why a madman's dream should be a Mission To Gehenna.